A Candlelight Ecstasy Romance ™

"You owe me," Wolf said.

His voice, cold as ice, sent a chill skipping down her spine.

"I owe you nothing," Micki whispered, astonished at his charge.

"You owe me one child. When you produce that child you may have your freedom. You're going to give me my legitimate child, so stop arguing and let's join the others in a toast to our marriage."

CANDLELIGHT ECSTASY ROMANCE™

Dear Reader:

In response to your enthusiasm for Candlelight Ecstasy Romances,™ we are now increasing the number of titles per month from two to three.

We are pleased to offer you sensuous novels set in America, depicting modern American women and men as they confront the provocative problems of a modern relationship.

Throughout the history of the Candlelight line, Dell has tried to maintain a high standard of excellence, to give you the finest in reading pleasure. It is now and will remain our most ardent ambition.

Vivian Stephens
Editor
Candlelight Romances

BREEZE
OFF THE
OCEAN

Amii Lorin

A CANDLELIGHT ECSTASY ROMANCE™

To my own Mickey—my sister,
whose faith is boundless as the sky.

To my own Bruce—my brother,
whose encouragement is constant as the sea.

Published by
Dell Publishing Co., Inc.
1 Dag Hammarskjold Plaza
New York, New York 10017

Dell ® TM 681510, Dell Publishing Co., Inc.

Candlelight Ecstasy Romance ™ is a trademark of
Dell Publishing Co., Inc., New York, New York.

ISBN: 0–440–10817–9

Printed in the United States of America

First printing—September 1981

CHAPTER 1

Micki's foot eased off the gas pedal as she drew alongside the toll booth of the Delaware Memorial Bridge. After tossing her coins into the exact-change catchall, she pressed down on the pedal to begin the climb over the high-girdered twin span. Even though she had actually just begun her journey, as soon as she'd left the bridge and had driven onto Route 40 she had the feeling of coming home.

In her mind she ticked off the names of the towns she'd drive through. Woodstown, Elmer, Malaga, Buena, Mays Landing.

"Mays Landing."

The softly murmured name brought a curl of excitement simply because from there it was a relatively short hop on Atlantic Route 559 to Sommers Point, then home. At the thought of the Point a small smile tugged at her soft, full lips. She had had fun at the Point, she and the group of kids she'd palled around with all those years ago.

One particular memory wiggled into her mind and her smile deepened. They had been playing a game of tag, she and seven other kids, when one of the boys—Benny Trent —had let out a loud yelp of pain and began hopping around on one foot. They had all laughed and jeered at him until they saw his great toe become scarlet with blood. As they crowded around him, Benny had dropped onto the sand, twisting his foot to get a closer look at the wound. A deep gash, inflicted by a jagged, half-buried clam shell, ran diagonally across the pad of his toe, bleeding profusely.

One of the other boys, a college student a few years older than the rest, had taken a Red Cross first aid course and, after examining the gash, declared that it would definitely need stitches.

Off to the hospital they went, en masse, laughing and joking to keep the pale Benny's spirits up.

"Boy, Benny," Cindy Langdon, Micki's best friend, had jeered. "How dumb can you get? Didn't your mother ever tell you you can get hurt if you go jumping up and down on a stupid clam shell?"

At the hospital Benny was led away to have the wound cleaned and stitched, and the rest of the children had camped, noisily, in the waiting room, much to the obvious exasperation of the hospital personnel.

When Benny returned, his toe almost twice its size from bandaging, the taunts and jokes began again.

Micki shook her head ruefully at how callous they'd all been, then brought her attention sharply alert as she drove through Woodstown's early afternoon traffic. After she left the town behind, the traffic was sparse and Micki allowed memory to have its way again.

She and the other kids hadn't been altogether heartless, she thought with amusement. For two weeks they had slavishly waited on Benny hand and foot and that bonehead, as Cindy called him, loved every minute of it.

That memory triggered off others and Micki laughed aloud on realizing Benny had usually been the target of their banter. In the case of Cindy, well, her gibes had been downright insulting. If, at that time, anyone would have told them that eventually Cindy would be married to Ben-

8

ny, they would all, Cindy included, have become hysterical. But, two years ago, that was exactly what had happened.

Micki had not been able to attend the wedding, as she'd been on the West Coast on a buying trip, but she had sent a lavish wedding gift, along with her surprised congratulations.

It would be good to see Cindy and Benny again, Micki mused, as she headed the little silver car straight as its namesake—Arrow—toward the coast. How many, Micki wondered, besides Cindy and Benny, had made their home there? Except for Cindy, Micki had completely lost touch with the rest of her gang.

There had been eight of them that traveled around together regularly. At intervals their number swelled, for beach parties and dances and the like, but the eight had remained constant from grade through high school. They were all of the same age, with one exception, Tony Menella, who had been two years their senior. It had been Tony who had advised Benny to have his toe stitched. Where was Tony now? Micki sighed. She simply didn't know. A small smile curved her lips at the thought that she'd probably find out where they all were before too long. Cindy would know not only where they were but what they were doing, as Cindy had always kept tabs on all of them.

Memories, one after the other, kept Micki company as she made her way steadily toward the coast. Growing-up memories, many happy, a few sad, invaded her mind. Only one did she push away, refuse to recognize. That one particular memory she had not looked at for a long time; she had no intention of doing so now.

The miles sped by, even more quickly after she'd turned onto Atlantic Route 559, and as she drove through Sommers Point she switched off the car's air-conditioner and wound down the window beside her. Excitement mounting, Micki passed the sign reading WELCOME TO OCEAN

CITY and at that instant a breeze off the ocean told her she was home.

Just getting across the Ninth Street Bridge was a project. In mid-July the influx of tourists added to the going-home-from-work crowd to make traffic a late afternoon nightmare. Undaunted, Micki inched along serenely. She loved the sound, the smells, everything about her hometown, and the traffic, compared to the suppertime crush around Wilmington, didn't bother her a bit.

Drinking in the sights avidly, Micki observed the number of people, mostly families, on the sidewalks, obviously coming from the beach, lugging beach chairs, umbrellas, and other beach paraphernalia, and shepherding youngsters. Micki knew that most were headed to apartments or motels, some to prepare dinner, others to bathe and dress before going out again to dine at one of the city's many fine restaurants or fast-food shops.

There were changes, of course, as there always were in a resort city, and Micki noted them automatically. At one place several well-remembered buildings had disappeared and at another a very classy new restaurant now presided. The changes did not fill her with dismay. On the contrary, she had grown up with changes and through it all the city basically remained the same. It was still a clean city. A city full of churches. A family-oriented resort city that was lovely to vacation in and equally lovely to grow up in. To Micki it would always be the same. Except for one brief visit, she had been away for six years, and yet it was the same. Home.

She turned off Ninth onto Wesley and after several blocks the traffic thinned out considerably. Two more turns and there was hardly any traffic at all. And then there was the house she was brought to four days after her birth.

How achingly familiar it was, with the lacy-leafed mimosa in the middle of the front lawn and the profuse banks of fuchsia and white azalea bushes on either side of

10

the front steps. Although she could see that the awnings were new, they were of exactly the same pattern as those that had always shaded the windows and large front porch.

With an emotional lump closing her throat, Micki turned the car onto the short driveway that ran along the side of the house and parked the car in front of the one-car garage at the end of the drive a short distance behind the house.

The soft whooshing sound of the kitchen screen door being pushed open came as she pulled on the hand brake.

"Micki!" Micki's father, Bruce Durrant, called as he strode along the flagstone path that led from the house to the garage. "Welcome home."

"Oh, Dad!" Micki flung the car door open and slid out into her father's arms. "It's so good to see you."

"Let me get a look at you." Grasping her arms, he leaned back, his eyes roving lovingly over her face. "You look more like your mother every time I see you," he murmured. "You've grown into a beautiful young woman, Micki."

"You wouldn't be just a tiny bit prejudiced, would you?" Micki laughed tremulously, blinking against the sudden hot sting in her eyes.

"Not in the least," Bruce denied firmly. "Your mother was an exceptionally lovely woman and you do look like her, maybe you're even more lovely."

Micki's eyes had been busy also and she noted the gray that now sprinkled her father's dark hair, the lines that radiated from his eyes, and the grooves from his nose to the corners of his mouth. Rather than distracting from his good looks, the signs of full maturity added character to his face and the silver among the dark strands of his hair lent a touch of distinction. Pleased with her perusal of him, Micki felt her smile widen.

"You look pretty good yourself, Mr. Durrant." Somehow the smile stayed in place. "How are you feeling?"

11

The hands grasping her shoulders gave her a little shake. "What a little worrywart you are." He chided softly. "I'm fine. Dr. Bassi assures me the ulcer is completely healed. I swear I haven't had a twinge of pain in months."

Micki's startlingly bright blue eyes gazed deeply into her father's dark brown ones. A sigh of relief escaped her lips at the happiness and contentment she found there. Happily Micki banished the memory of the panic and fear she'd experienced the night Regina had called her. God! What a horrible night that had been. Regina's voice, tight with fear, waking her with the news of her father's collapse with a perforated ulcer. Fighting the terror of the unknown, Micki had driven through the silent pre-dawn hours with a strangely icy composure. Thankfully, for Regina had been on the verge of falling apart, Micki's composure had lasted through the following nerve-racking two days, but after Dr. Bassi had told them that her father was out of danger, Micki had gone to her old room and relieved her anxiety by sobbing into her pillow.

Now, satisfied with the obvious signs of his glowing good looks and well-being, Micki gave him another quick hug. With her absorption in the most important man in her life, Micki didn't hear the repeated whoosh of the kitchen screen door.

"Are you two going to stand here in the driveway the whole two weeks of Micki's vacation?" Micki's stepmother, Regina, teased.

Micki's entire body tensed at the sound of Regina's velvety, throaty voice, then she made herself relax. What was past was past, she admonished herself sharply, and best forgotten. With unstudied grace, she swung her small slim frame out of her father's embrace, one hand reaching out to take the pale one Regina had extended.

"Hello, Regina." Micki was slightly amazed at the even tenor of her voice. "No need to ask how you are; you look fantastic, as ever."

It was true. At thirty-nine Regina was as exotically

12

beautiful as she had been when she had married Bruce Durrant at twenty-five, the exact same age that Micki was now. Her glossy black hair, worn smoothed back off her face in an intricately curved twist, was completely free of silver. Her pale-complexioned, unbelievably beautiful face was completely free of any sign of encroaching age. And her tall frame was still willowy, completely free of any unsightly bulges. And that voice! Oh, the hours a very young, twelve-year-old Micki had spent trying, unsuccessfully, to emulate that voice. Even today, as then, Micki had no idea of how pleasing to the ear her own soft, somewhat husky, voice was.

"You do not look the same," Regina returned easily. Then, to Micki's surprise, she echoed her husband's words of a few minutes ago. "You grow more like your mother every time I see you, and everyone knows how lovely she was."

Micki managed to hide her startled reaction to Regina's compliment in the general confusion of collecting her suitcases and getting them into the house.

Regina trailed behind Micki and her father as they lugged the valises to her bedroom and lingered after Bruce left the room with a promise of a pre-dinner drink for Micki as soon as she'd settled in.

"Micki?"

Micki's hand stilled in the act of unlocking her largest suitcase at the hesitant, uncertain note in her stepmother's voice. Features composed, Micki turned to gaze at Regina. "Yes?"

"Do you suppose we could possibly be friends now?"

Regina's tone had smoothed out, but an anxious expression still clouded her beautiful black eyes.

"Do you?"

As soon as they were out of her mouth Micki wished the words unspoken. Why, she chided herself, hadn't she simply said yes and let the whole sorry business remain buried?

13

"I would like to try," Regina answered quietly. "I have always liked you." At Micki's slightly raised eyebrows, Regina stated firmly, "Yes, I have. And there is no reason now why we shouldn't be friends. I think you'll find I'm not quite the same person since your father's near brush with death. It's sad, but I nearly had to lose him to realize —well—just exactly how foolishly I was behaving."

"Regina, you do not have to—" Micki began, but Regina seemed determined to have her say.

"You were very patient with and kind to me while your father was so very ill, even though you were nearly out of your mind with worry yourself. I have not forgotten that and I never will." Regina paused, as if uncertain how to continue, and then, with a light shrug of her elegant shoulders, she plunged on forcefully. "I love your father very much, I always have. Yes, really," she vowed as Micki's brows rose again. "The only explanation, or excuse, I have for my previous behavior is his neglect of me—due solely to business pressures, I admit—after our marriage and my selfish reaction to that neglect."

"Regina, please—"

"No, Micki, let me finish," Regina insisted. "When we married, your father was a very handsome and charming man, as indeed he still is, and I wanted to be the only important thing in his life, even to the exclusion of an eleven-year-old child."

"I remember," Micki inserted, then felt petty at Regina's wince. And yet, she defended herself silently, she *did* remember, painfully.

"Yes, of course you remember," Regina went on doggedly. "That's why I must say all this, clear the air between us." Again she paused, wet her lips nervously. "From the time I was fourteen I was aware of my attraction to the opposite sex and I used that attraction to punish your father. It was foolish and immature, I know, but I realize now that at the time I *was* foolish and immature. I—I had to almost lose Bruce before I woke up to

14

my own stupidity." She closed her eyes briefly and when she opened them again her lashes glistened with teardrops.

For several long moments the two women stared at each other. Micki's eyes, carefully veiled, revealed nothing of what she was feeling. Regina's eyes held mute appeal. Slowly, as if gathering strength, Regina drew a deep breath.

"And now, about that incident six years ago," Regina said softly.

No! No! a voice screamed inside Micki's head. What came out of her parched lips was a strangled whisper.

"No, Regina. I do not want to talk about that."

Regina's eyes flickered with alarm and her tone dropped to a murmur of self-reproachment.

"Oh, God, it still hurts you." One pale hand was extended, as if in supplication. "Oh, my dear, I had no idea the pain went so deep. How can you ever forgive me?"

Micki was saved from answering by the sound of her father's strong, impatient call from the bottom of the stairway.

"What in the world are you two women doing up there?" His tone took on a mock petulant edge. "I'm getting very lonely down here all by myself."

Regina's head snapped around to the bedroom's open doorway, then swung back to Micki.

"I'm sorry," she whispered. "Please believe that. I— I—" She shook her head and cleared her throat. "We better go down. Leave the unpacking, I'll help you with it later."

Forcing her stiff facial muscles into relaxation, Micki left the room, and Regina's line of conversation, gratefully, silently determined that that particular subject would not be brought up again during her visit.

Surprisingly, or maybe not too surprisingly, with the air between the two women somewhat cleared, the evening passed pleasantly.

During dinner Micki brought her father and Regina up

to date on her activities, saving the most important detail for last. They had carried their coffee into the living room and as Micki sipped at her creamy brew with a contented sigh, the only indication she gave as to the import of her news was an added sparkle in her usually bright blue eyes.

"Oh, by the way," Micki drawled diffidently. "Just before I left the shop for this vacation I was informed I was being promoted to head buyer."

A short silence followed her casually tossed statement, a silence that revealed to Micki exactly how aware her father and Regina were of the importance of her announcement.

After leaving the small college, where she had been studying business merchandising, so precipitously only six weeks into her second year, Micki had considered herself fortunate in acquiring the job of salesclerk in a very exclusive ladies' boutique, which was located in the lobby of one of the largest, most prestigious hotels in Wilmington. It was not the job of salesclerk that excited Micki, but the knowledge that the boutique was just one of a large chain of similar shops that ranged along the entire East Coast. When she had been interviewed for the job by the shop's manager, a tall, slim woman in her mid-forties, Micki had been informed that due to the size of the independently owned chain, the chance for advancement was excellent for anyone who did not object to relocating. Micki had been quick to assure the somewhat aristocratic woman that she had no objections at all to relocating, as Wilmington was not her hometown.

It had taken time and much hard work on Micki's part, but eventually the promotions did come and for the last eighteen months she had been assistant buyer for the Wilmington shop. And now—could it have been only yesterday?—this latest promotion.

"Micki, that's wonderful!" her father exclaimed, jumping out of his chair to come across the room and bestow a huge hug on her. "Congratulations."

"And you haven't heard the best part yet," Micki gasped laughingly when he'd released his crushing hold. "The position is for the Atlantic City store."

"Atlantic City?" Bruce repeated softly, then he nearly shouted. "Honey, that means you can move home."

Still laughing, Micki nodded her head. Totally absorbed in each other, both Micki and her father had completely forgotten Regina. In the old days Regina would have made her presence known forcefully, now the voice that penetrated their euphoria was soft, hesitant.

"May I add my congratulations to your father's, Micki?"

"Oh, Regina, I'm sorry," Micki murmured contritely. "Of course you may."

"Yes, darling," Bruce inserted, one arm encircling his wife's waist to draw her close. "Of course you may. We're a family." He paused an instant before adding, "Aren't we?"

A quick glance of understanding and truce passed between the two women.

"Yes, Dad," Micki agreed firmly. "We are a family."

Regina's black eyes spoke eloquently of her relief and thanks and Micki was amazed at the feeling of peace that washed over her. For the most part the fourteen years of her father's second marriage had been turbulent and Micki greeted the cessation of hostilities with a silent prayer of thanks. Still, she didn't want to strain the ties of this newfound accord, so she tacked on with equal firmness, "But I'll be looking for my own apartment."

"In Atlantic City?"

Bruce and Regina spoke in astonished unison and Micki fully understood the reason for their astonishment. It was a well-known fact that living accommodations in Atlantic City were almost as hard to find as brontosaurus teeth since the influx of the big hotels with their gambling casinos. The added fact that the shop Micki would be working in was located in one of those hotels lent a sprinkling of

17

spice to her excitement. Now she hastened to correct their impression.

"No, not in Atlantic City, here in Ocean City. Atlantic City's such a short run up the coast I doubt it will take me any longer to get to work from here than it did in the early morning crush in Wilmington."

"The way I understand it," Bruce said quietly, "there are already quite a few people that are employed by the hotels making their home here." He hesitated, his eyes mirroring his sadness. "But why do you want to look for an apartment? Why can't you stay here at home?"

"Oh, Dad." Micki smiled weakly. "I've been on my own for almost six years now. I'm used to having my own place. I've got an apartment full of furniture and things I've acquired over those six years." Her smile deepened, became impish. "But I have made arrangements to have my stuff packed and sent here in the interim—if you don't mind?"

"Mind?" Bruce echoed. "Of course we don't mind."

"Not at all." Regina seconded her husband's words.

"Oh, sure." Micki's laughter rippled through the comfortable room. "But wait until you have all my stuff dumped onto your doorstep. You may wish you'd given a very firm no."

Regina made fresh coffee and the three of them settled around the kitchen table to make plans and discuss the pros and cons of various areas in which Micki might be interested in apartment hunting. During the course of the discussion the section of the city in which Cindy and Benny lived came up and at the mention of the young couple's name the topic of the conversation veered to them.

"I haven't seen either of them since they made final settlement on the house," Bruce told Micki. "But Cindy did call me at the office after they'd moved in, to again thank me for finding the property for them and inform me that they were absolutely thrilled with it." He grinned

18

broadly. "Those last words are an exact quote from Cindy."

"Sounds so much like her I can almost hear her voice," Micki grinned back. Her father owned a flourishing real estate business and it pleased her to know Cindy had gone to him when she was ready to buy a home. "It will be wonderful to see Cindy and Benny again."

"Did they know you were coming home?" Regina asked. "And that you'll be staying?"

Micki was shaking her head before Regina had finished speaking. "No, I wanted to surprise them," Micki answered. Then her eyes shifted to rest lovingly on her father. "Besides which, I wanted my first evening at home to be free of interruptions."

The answering look of love in her father's eyes and the understanding smile on Regina's lips deepened the feeling of well-being inside Micki. Stifling a yawn behind her hand, she pushed her chair away from the table and stood up.

"I'm going to have a shower then go to bed." Another yawn was unsuccessfully hidden. When Regina moved to get up, Micki shook her head at her. "You don't have to come up, Regina. I can finish my unpacking in the morning." After kissing her father lightly on the cheek, she wished them both a good night and swung out of the room.

Alone in her bedroom Micki stood still just inside the door and let her eyes roam slowly over familiar things. Everything was the same as she'd left it. Even the paint on the walls, though fresh, was the same bright daffodil yellow as it had always been. When her eyes touched the double, leather-bound picture frame sitting on the nightstand by the bed, they stopped. Her gaze unwavering, Micki walked across the room and picked up the frame.

The picture on one side was an enlargement of a snapshot that had been taken on the front lawn. Three figures stood under a mimosa tree. Micki's mother was turned slightly from the camera as she smiled up at her husband, and between them Micki, at age six, her favorite doll clutched in her arms, grinned impishly at the camera. The picture had been snapped by a close friend of her mother's the summer before her mother's death in a fiery highway accident.

Micki blinked over hot tears before shifting her gaze to the other side of the frame. It had been years since she'd really looked at the studio portrait of her mother and now, remembering her father's words when she arrived, she studied the color shot carefully before lifting her eyes to her own reflection in the dressing-table mirror opposite the bed. Yes, the well-defined features were very similar: a slim, straight nose; high, though not prominent, cheek-bones; softly rounded chin, although Micki's did have a more determined cast. If the color in the photo was true, they shared the same bright blue eyes and fair skin tone. But her mother's hair, worn long and smooth at the time, was a gleaming auburn with deep red highlights, whereas Micki's, which she wore short in an attempt to control her loose, unruly curls, was a dark chestnut. Yes, there were similarities, but her mother had been beautiful, and in Micki's own opinion, she was not.

With a brief, what-does-it-matter shrug, Micki replaced the frame, then stood eyeing her suitcases dispassionately. Sighing softly, she flicked the clasps of the largest case and opened the valise. Do it now, she told herself firmly, or everything will be crushed beyond wearing.

Micki kicked off her sandals and moved silently over the plush, gold wall-to-wall carpeting as she placed her clothes in the closet and drawers. When the bags were empty, Micki placed them against the wall beside the bedroom door for storage in the large hall closet in the morning, then turned back to the room, a tiny smile of satisfaction tugging at her lips. Everything about the room satisfied her.

Her father had given her carte blanche in decorating it

20

when she was sixteen, and now, nine years later, everything about the room still pleased her. Micki's eyes sparkled as they skimmed the white wicker headboard, chair, low table, and clothes hamper. A stroke of genius that, she thought smugly. Who would have thought, nine years ago, that wicker would become so popular, not to mention expensive.

Humming softly she slipped out of her white denim slacks and pulled her blue-and-white striped shirt over her head. Her lacy bra and filmy bikini briefs followed her slacks and shirt into the hamper. She put on a terry robe, pulled the belt tight, scooped up a short, sheer nightie, and made for the bathroom for a quick shower.

Micki was patting her five-foot-two frame dry when she heard her father and Regina come up the stairs and go into their room. Gritting her teeth, she mentally clamped a lid on the flash of remembered pain and resentment the sound of their bedroom door closing sent through her. Always that sound, by the very intimate connotations it conjured, had had the power to hurt her, make her feel cut off from her father, bereft. Now she pushed those feelings away. You're a full-grown woman, she told herself sternly, with a full, rich life of your own. Go to bed, go to sleep, what's done is done and can't be changed. Forget it.

Minutes after she'd returned to her room, there was a soft tap on her door. Thinking it was her father coming to wish her a second good night, Micki called, "Come in," without hesitation, then wished she hadn't when she saw it was Regina. Fearing a repeat of their earlier conversation, Micki tried to forestall the older woman.

"Whatever it is, Regina"—Micki faked a huge yawn—"could it wait until morning? I can hardly keep my eyes open."

Regina bit her bottom lip nervously, hesitated, then drew a deep, courage-gathering breath.

"Micki, I don't want to upset you, please believe that,

21

but"—she drew another, shorter breath before rushing on—"we must talk about Wolf."

"No!"

The one word escaped through Micki's lips like a muffled explosion and she flinched as if the other woman had actually struck her.

"But you don't understand." Regina's tone held a pleading note. "We must discuss this, he's—"

"Regina." Micki's voice was low, intense with warning. "This is still my room. I'm asking you to please leave it so I can go to bed."

"But Wolf—"

"Regina." Micki's teeth were clenched in an effort to control her voice. "You asked me earlier if we can be friends. Well, I'm willing to try, but there is one condition. I cannot, *will* not, discuss that person. Not now, not ever."

"Oh, Micki," Regina sighed. "You don't understand."

"And I don't want to," Micki snapped. "Do you want me to leave this house in the morning? Find a motel room until I can get an apartment?"

"No!" Regina exclaimed in alarm. "Of course not. Your father would—"

"Well, then." Micki didn't wait to hear what her father would do. "The subject will remain closed and forgotten. As long as Dad looks as well and happy as he does now, I'm content to meet you halfway toward friendship. I fully expect you to do the same. Do you get my meaning?"

Regina's eyes closed briefly in defeat and she nodded. Before staring directly into Micki's eyes, she murmured, "But please don't say I didn't try."

Micki wondered over those parting words several minutes after Regina left the room. What in the world could she have meant? With a shrug of her shoulders she turned toward the bed, then stopped and became very still, the echo of that name searing through her mind.

Wolf.

Wolf—a predatory animal's name that suited perfectly the predatory human male. A mental picture formed and, her face twisted with pain, Micki pushed it from her mind.

Damn, damn, damn Regina, for saying that name out loud.

Memories crowded in threatening to overwhelm her. Shaking herself like a wet dog, Micki moved jerkily to the bed. No, she would not allow the memories to gather, collect in her mind. Forcing herself to stand very still beside the bed, she breathed deeply. In. Out. In. Out.

"I must call Cindy."

In. Out. In. Out.

"I must go apartment hunting."

In. Out. In. Out.

"I must run up to Atlantic City and check out the shop, introduce myself."

In. Out. In. Out.

"I've controlled these emotions before, I will tonight."

Doing the breathing exercise, speaking softly, Micki felt the pain recede, the trembling leave her body. After what seemed a very long time she slipped between the bedsheets, closed her eyes, and cried as if her heart were broken.

CHAPTER 2

The next morning Micki woke early, refreshed and ready to face a new day. Surprisingly, after her violent crying bout, she had slept deeply. The realization that she had once again won the battle against her memories added to the feeling of well-being her uninterrupted rest had instilled.

Glancing at the bedside clock, she sat up quickly and slipped off the bed; if she hurried she could have breakfast with her father. She thrust her arms into her robe and left her room at a near run, dashed into the bathroom to splash cold water on her face and brush her teeth, then hurried back along the hall and down the stairs.

"Morning." Micki breezed into the kitchen and planted a kiss on her father's smooth, freshly shaven cheek before seating herself at the old-fashioned wooden table.

"Morning, princess."

Micki's perfect white teeth flashed in a grin of delight at her father's use of the pet name. It had been years since he'd called her that, and she loved the sound of it.

"I thought you'd sleep in this morning." Bruce grinned back before adding, "What got you awake so early? Regina and I didn't wake you, did we?"

"No." Micki shook her head emphatically. "I must have been slept out." She smiled her thanks as Regina placed a glass of juice in front of her. "I'm used to getting up early, you know."

"All the more reason to sleep in when you get the chance," Bruce replied placidly. "Regina's scrambling eggs—would you like some?"

"No, thank you." Micki's mild grimace drew a chuckle from her dad.

"Kids!" The soft exclamation took the sting from his word. "Who can figure them out? You always loved eggs for breakfast until that last year you were in college."

Micki's stomach seemed to turn over and for a moment she felt trapped while she raked her mind for a reply. Thankfully neither her father nor Regina noticed the way her face had paled, as their attention was occupied by Regina serving the eggs.

"I guess I just got tired of them," Micki finally managed weakly, eyeing the creamy yellow mound on the plates.

"Just like that." Bruce snapped his fingers. "It doesn't make sense."

"Stop teasing, Bruce." Unknowingly, Regina saved Micki from the effort of finding a more plausible excuse. "As youngsters mature, their tastes change." As she sat down at the table, Regina offered Micki a tentative smile. "Don't mind your father, Micki. He's in a very good but devilish mood this morning, due, I'm sure, to your being home again."

The grin her father flashed at her confirmed Regina's words. A slow, silent sigh fluttered through Micki's lips as she returned Regina's smile.

"I can see"—Micki deliberately lowered her voice conspiratorially—"you and I are going to have to stick together to keep this feisty man in line."

Bruce's head snapped up from his plate, his glance sharp between the two women. The spark of hope that had entered his eyes seemed to grow into wonderment as he

26

studied first his daughter's then his wife's friendly expressions.

Micki fully understood the almost breathless stillness that seemed to grip him. The two women had been opponents, at first silent and then very vocal, since the day Bruce married Regina. He had coaxed, cajoled, and even ordered Micki to make more of an effort at getting along with her stepmother. The only thing he'd achieved was to fill Micki with a deeper sense of resentment. She had made an attempt at friendship with Regina. At the very vulnerable age of eleven she had welcomed the idea of a mother. Regina, a younger, beautiful Regina, had quickly disabused her of that idea. Without actually saying the words, Regina had left little doubt in Micki's young mind of exactly where she stood. If Micki wanted her father's attention, she would have to fight for it. Micki had fought silently but bitterly, and until last night, she had thought it was a battle she could never win.

Now the gentle smile Micki gave her father erased the doubt lingering around the edges of his expression. She saw him swallow with difficulty and the action brought a corresponding lump to her throat. Shifting her eyes, she caught the quick flutter of Regina's lashes and the lump grew in size.

"Princess," Bruce murmured solemnly, "I wonder if you realize how happy I am to have you home." The slight emphasis he placed on the word *home* told the full story.

"And you can have no idea how happy it makes me to be home." Micki let her own emphasis reflect his before she laughed a little shakily. "And if you don't eat your breakfast, you are going to be late for work."

"Oh, but you see"—Bruce followed her lead in lightening the mood—"that's the fun part of being the boss. I can breeze in and out of the office whenever I please." He paused, a mock frown creasing his forehead. "The only thing is, as I have a very important client coming this morning, I damned well better please to get moving."

After her father had left for the office and Regina had refused her offer to help with the dishes, Micki went to the phone in the living room to call Cindy.

"Hello." Cindy's bubbly voice sang across the wire after the fourth ring.

"Hi, Cindy, how are you?"

"Micki!" The exclamation was like a small explosion. "Where are you? Are you here in Ocean City? How are you? When did you get home? Are you home?" The questions followed each other in such rapid succession Micki laughingly shouted to get a word in.

"Cindy, if you will take time to breathe, I'll explain the wheres and whys." The small silence that followed these words allowed Micki to continue briefly. "I am home, yes, and—"

"Then don't bother to go any further," Cindy broke in. "Jump in your car and come to the house, I'm dying to see you." She hesitated, then asked apologetically, "Or did you have other plans for this morning?"

"As a matter of fact," Micki laughed, "my only plans for today were to come and see you, if you had no other plans. Does that make any sense at all?"

"Perfect sense," Cindy declared happily. "So why are you still on the phone? Get truckin'." She hung up before Micki could even tell her she would.

Still smiling, Micki went to the kitchen to tell Regina where she was going, adding she had no idea when she'd be back.

"Oh, that will work out perfectly." Regina's smile was still somewhat tentative. "I have a lunch date with Betty Grant and we'd planned to do some shopping after lunch. How is Cindy feeling now?"

The question startled Micki, wiped the smile off her face.

"She sounded fine," she answered slowly, then asked anxiously, "Why? Has she been ill?"

"No, no," Regina soothed. "Not ill, but she did have a

28

few bad moments at the beginning of her pregnancy, you know."

Everything inside Micki seemed to freeze with an emotion she couldn't begin to put a name to. Cindy pregnant? Why hadn't she told her?

Regina glanced up from the dish she was drying; her face grew puzzled at Micki's stillness. "Is something wrong?" she asked with concern.

"No." Micki shook her head and forced the smile back to her stiff lips. "I—I didn't know Cindy was pregnant."

"Didn't know?" For a second Regina's eyes were totally blank, then they widened with dismay. "Oh, damn," she groaned. "Cindy must have wanted to surprise you and now I've ruined it for her."

"You couldn't know, and I'll play dumb when she tells me." Micki wet her parched lips as she turned toward the doorway. "Cindy will have her surprise." Moving swiftly through the doorway, she added, "I'll see you when I see you."

Inside her room Micki leaned back against the door and closed her eyes, a soft moan catching at her throat. Hugging her midriff tightly as if to contain the pain inside, she dug her teeth into her lower lip. For a few moments the remembered torment was so real she wanted to cry out against it. Oh, God, she thought sickly, would the hurt never go away? Breathing deeply, exactly as she had the night before, she forced herself to a measure of calmness. She had to get dressed, go see Cindy, and act surprised and happy about her pregnancy. She was happy for Cindy.

By the time Micki backed her car out of the driveway, she had her emotions under control. Driving slowly through the mid-morning traffic, she glanced around quickly. The tourist season was in full swing. People of all ages, shapes, and sizes were on their way to the beach. Cyclists pedaled their way toward their destination. The streets were crowded with cars; people coming into the city, people going out of the city, and some just driving

29

around the city pursuing their business, and over all, the gulls soared and dipped and sang their raucous songs. Micki loved it. She always had and as she drove through it she felt the stiffness ease out of her body.

It was not a very long drive, as the house Cindy and Benny had bought was located just south of where the long boardwalk ended. From Cindy's letters Micki knew it was a double unit building fronting the beach and ocean. The reason the young couple decided to buy a double unit was the obvious one: the increasing cost of real estate. The summer rental on the apartment made up half of the yearly mortgage payments. The cost of the building had been exorbitant but, Cindy had written, for a place of their own, it had been worth it.

Cindy was waiting at the door, and as soon as Micki drove onto the crushed-stone driveway, she pushed the car door open and ran to meet her.

After incoherent greetings and fierce hugs were exchanged, the two women stood back to examine each other, identical smiles of pleasure on their faces. Extending a slim hand, Micki placed it gently on the bulge that was Cindy's belly.

"I'm so happy for you," she said softly. "But, why didn't you tell me?"

"I wanted to surprise you." Cindy laughed. "If you remember, you wrote that you were thinking of spending your vacation at home this year and, well, I just wanted to see your face when you saw me."

"You nit." Micki shook her head in mock reproach. "Was my expression worth keeping the secret all this time?"

"Well worth it," Cindy affirmed, taking her arm and leading her to the house. "You looked absolutely stunned."

A mental picture of how she'd reacted to the news a short time ago allowed Micki to answer with complete honesty. "I assure you I was. When is the big event slated to happen?"

"Around Christmastime," Cindy replied happily. "Oh, Micki, don't you think that's exciting? I mean, a baby for Christmas."

"Very exciting," Micki murmured. She stepped over the threshold directly into a large, airy living room, resplendent with plants of all kinds, a half dozen of which hung from the ceiling.

The apartment was larger than Micki would have expected. In addition to the living room there was a tiny dining room, a roomy kitchen, one and a half baths, and three bedrooms, one of which was in the process of redecoration.

"The baby's room," Cindy explained needlessly.

"I love it," Micki enthused honestly. "All of it. And the fact that it's practically right on the beach makes it worth whatever you paid for it."

"That's what we thought," Cindy nodded. "Of course we don't know what it will be like in the winter, but we're delighted with it just the same."

They wandered back into the kitchen and from there onto the wide, awning-covered deck.

"I thought since it's so hot already this morning, we'd have lunch out here."

"Wonderful." Micki stared entranced at the view of the beach and sun-sparkled ocean the deck afforded. "Oh, Cindy," she breathed softly, "this place was worth almost any amount of money, just for the view."

"I know—it's super." Cindy laughed. "Benny and I have breakfast out here every nice morning."

"How is Benny?" Micki asked belatedly. "And how does he feel about becoming a father?"

"He's fine." Cindy smiled softly. "And he's so excited about the baby he can hardly wait." The smile grew into a grin. "We were shopping last week and would you believe I had to drag him out of the sports department? He wanted to buy the baby a football, for heaven's sake."

"Knowing Benny, I can believe it." Micki grinned back. "Do you think most men get a little soft in the head about their first child?"

Micki didn't even hear Cindy's answer, for suddenly she felt like a large hand was squeezing all the air from her chest. Dear God, why did the most innocent remarks still have the power to hurt her like this?

Cindy laughed and pulling herself together, Micki managed to laugh with her. The sudden explosion of air eased the constriction of her lungs, and as the conversation switched to the more immediate subject of lunch, Micki felt her emotional gear shift back into normal.

By the time they had finished their melon and gone on to small salads and cold chicken sandwiches Micki was glad she'd decided on a spaghetti-strapped sundress that morning. The July sun was brassy in a cloud-free blue sky. Even with the sea breeze wafting under the awning, by one o'clock the heat drove them indoors.

By the time Cindy had filled Micki in on the comings and goings of their friends and Micki had imparted her own news about her job and her plans to make her home permanently in Ocean City, most of the afternoon was gone.

After agreeing to have dinner with Cindy and Benny one evening, Micki left, cautioning Cindy to get plenty of rest to combat the enervating effects of the heat.

Driving through the shimmery heat waves that rose from the street, Micki reflected on what Cindy had told her about their mutual friends. They had really scattered —one as far away as Alaska. But Tony Menella was back. After finishing college, he had gone to work for a large advertising firm in Trenton, but a little over a year ago he'd packed it in and come home. He was working in Atlantic City, but he was living in Ocean City, much the same as Micki herself would now be doing.

32

Into her own thoughts, she stopped at an intersection when a car cut in front of her and, glancing up, let her gaze skim over the area. Idly she studied a new motel on the opposite corner. Very classy, she was thinking when she was startled alert by the opening of her passenger side door.

"What in the—!" Micki began, head swinging around. The words shriveled on her lips as she saw a long, lean frame settle into the seat next to her and felt the impact of the odd, silver-gray eyes of Wolf Renninger.

"It's safe to drive on now."

The soft, taunting words broke through the shock gripping her mind and by reflex Micki started the car.

Her mental process was set into motion at the same time. Anger searing her mind, she glanced around sharply for a parking space. She wasn't hauling his carcass anywhere.

"Pull into this lot here." The taunting edge to his tone was more pronounced, as if he'd read her thoughts and was amused by them.

Gritting her teeth, Micki glanced in the direction he'd indicated and saw it was the parking lot belonging to the motel she'd been looking at.

"But I can't park on that lot it's—"

"It's all right," Wolf interrupted, "I work there."

Angrily Micki spun the wheel and drove the car onto the lot, following his terse directions to a section marked EMPLOYEES PARKING—PRIVATE. The moment the car was stationary Micki turned to face him, blue eyes shooting bright sparks of anger.

"Now just what do you think you're doing?"

"Hello, Micki." Wolf's soft voice laughed at her. "It's been a long time."

"Not nearly long enough," Micki snapped acidly. "Why did you get into the car? What do you want?"

The smile that curved his sometimes hard, always sensuous lips sent a shiver racing along Micki's spine and she

33

gripped the steering wheel to keep her hands from trembling.

"I want to talk to you," Wolf replied smoothly. "And look at you."

"You've had your look," she said sharply. It was true. From the minute he'd entered the car his eyes had clung to her face like a beauty mask and it was making her very edgy. "So talk."

"Not here, it's too hot and I'd hate to see you melt all over the upholstery." That unnerving smile touched his mouth briefly. "Come with me, I have an apartment in the complex." The taunting laugh came back into his tone. "Or are you afraid?"

"Afraid of you?" Micki knew it was foolish to accept his challenge, but she also knew she had to prove something to him—and herself. Swinging open her car door with a flourish, she quipped, "Lead the way to your lair, Wolf. Or is it den?"

His soft laughter did strange things to her equilibrium, and for that reason only she allowed him the liberty of taking her arm.

He led her through a side entrance into the motel lobby, which was lavishly decorated in a south-seas motif, past the curious stares of the two men behind the reception desk, and up the curving stairway. As she mounted the last step, Micki barely had time to register the fact that the stairs opened onto what appeared to be a short crosswalk that connected two sections of the motel for, without pausing, Wolf turned right along the short crosswalk to where it connected with a long hallway. At the junction he turned left and strode along the hallway to the very end. The only difference between the door he unlocked and all the others that faced each other along the hall was the absence of a number.

The door opened into a fair-sized living room, but what caught Micki's attention, and her breath, was a large picture window on the far wall. From that height the window

34

gave a panoramic view of beachfront and ocean. Without a word Micki entered the deliciously cool room and crossed the plush bronze carpeting to stare out the window. Micki was not unlike numerous other people as to the hypnotic effect the movement of the ocean had on the emotions. But Wolf's quiet voice jerked her out of her mesmeric state.

"Would you like a drink?"

The arched look she threw him drew his soft mocking laughter.

"A soft drink?" he chided. "Iced tea? Perrier?"

"Do you have lime?"

"Yes."

"Perrier with lime then, please."

Micki watched him as he went around the waist-high wooden bookshelves that divided the living room from the kitchen. While he went about the business of getting the drinks, she made a quick inventory of him. He had changed, matured, as she had herself and the change was heart stopping. He had been good-looking at thirty. Now, at thirty-six, life had left its stamp on him.

The square, determined jawline now proclaimed iron control. His golden tan skin stretched shiny and smooth over his long straight nose, his high cheekbones, and the angular planes of his face. The silver-gray eyes, arched over by thick, dark brows, now held a calculating sharpness. He wore his dark brown hair short in back, but its wavy thickness was completely intact. And his six-foot-plus frame, never thick, had pared down to the lean, sinewy look of the predator whose name he bore. One would not call him merely good-looking now. There were any number of adjectives one might apply, ranging from devastating to dangerous. One might even add slightly cruel-looking, but never merely good-looking.

Micki caught herself following his every move, a breathless sort of excitement clutching her throat at the sheer masculine look of him. *Don't be an idiot,* she told herself

35

harshly. *Play it cool. Play it safe. He's trouble, pure un-adulterated trouble, and no one knows it better than you.*

Casting her eyes away in search of something more worthy of her appraisal, she fastened on the living room. Masculine to the point of Spartan, Micki was surprised to find she really liked the effect the warm earth tones of bronze, brown, and gold, with a splash of green here and there lent the room. He probably didn't have a thing to do with the decor, she decided disparagingly. *I'll bet every room in the motel is decorated in the same way.*

"Like it?"

His quiet voice, startlingly close to her ear, made her jump. His next words brought a tinge of pink to her cheeks. "I decorated it myself." He cocked his head to one side as his eyes roamed the room. "Personally, I think I did a damned good job."

"Oh, I'm sure it's perfectly suitable"—Micki waved her hand carelessly—"for a man."

"You've grown up." The simple statement was issued as he handed her her drink. "Grown more beautiful too." The rider was accompanied by that disquieting, sensuous smile. He lifted his glass to her in a mock salute and Micki's brows arched at the amber-colored liquid it contained.

"A little too hot for the hard stuff in the middle of the day, isn't it?" she asked bitingly.

"I've yet to be flattened by a single glass of bourbon and water." His silvery eyes roamed insolently over her face and body. "It takes something a little more heady to put me flat."

She was perfectly well aware of what that something was. A warm female body, any warm female body. She lifted her chin and stared him straight in the eye. "You said you wanted to talk to me," she elucidated clearly. "What about?"

"About how you are." Wolf's voice had dropped an octave. He moved closer to her and she didn't like having

36

to tilt her head back to look up into his face. His voice went lower.

"About what you've been doing."

"I'm fine." Micki's throat felt parched and she took several deep swallows of her lime-flavored water before adding, "I've been working."

Long, hard-looking fingers began teasing the bow on her dress straps and a remembered chill of pleasure feathered her arms. Micki opened her mouth to tell Wolf to stop as she lifted her head. The words and her breath dried up in her mouth. He had lowered his head and his face was so close she could smell the pungent aroma of bourbon. Now his voice was so low she wasn't sure for a moment that she heard him correctly.

"About who you're sleeping with."

For a full five seconds she stood stunned, then indignation kicked fury through her veins and retaliation from her mouth.

"That's none of your business!" She spun away from him, setting her drink down on a glass-topped table as she headed for the door. Hand on the knob, she turned back to him, eyes glittering with anger.

"But of one thing you may be sure—he's not already tied, legally, to another."

Micki turned the knob and pulled the door open. The palm of Wolf's hand hit the solid wood forcefully, slamming it shut again. Micki stood perfectly still, almost afraid to breathe. The quietness of his tone unnerved rather than calmed her.

"What, exactly, is that last dig supposed to mean?"

While he spoke he turned her around and forced her face up to look at him. Micki flattened herself against the door, hating the havoc the look of him and the scent of him created within her. His hard, taunting mouth was too close. Alarm vied with a sudden, urgent need to feel the touch of that mouth. Alarm won, sending her tone to sub-zero.

"I'm not a fool, Wolf." With effort she managed to not only meet but hold his intent gaze. "I never was the complete fool you thought I was."

"I never thought you were a fool," Wolf denied sternly. He loomed over her, his head lowering until his mouth was no more than a sigh away. "Baby, baby," he murmured hoarsely. "Why did you run from me?"

"Why?" Somehow she pushed a dry laugh from her throat. "Because this fool suddenly smartened up and realized what she didn't want."

His lips caught, played with hers. "Tell me now you didn't want this." His hands came up to grasp her hips, arch her close to him. Moving slowly, caressingly, they reached over her waist, settled possessively over her breasts. "Or this," he groaned into her mouth. When he felt her shudder, his hands moved again, long fingers encircling her throat while his thumbs stroked her collarbones. His breathing ragged, he rasped, "Or this," as his mouth crushed hers.

For one blinding instant everything inside Micki urged her to surrender. Then reason, plus a dash of self-preservation, took over and she went as cold and unresponsive as a stone.

Wolf didn't force the issue. Within seconds of her withdrawal he lifted his head and stepped back.

"I haven't the vaguest idea what you've been talking about." His silvery eyes had a dangerous, calculating gleam. "But I intend to find out."

"Don't waste your time beating a dead horse," Micki choked out. She wet her lips and felt her heart thump when his eyes dropped to her mouth. Pushing her words a little, she went on. "When something's dead, it's dead. And what happened between us died a long time ago."

"Prove it."

He rapped the words at her so fast she blinked in confusion.

"Prove it?" she repeated indignantly. "It doesn't have to be proven. It's evident."

"Not to me." His tone was hard and unyielding. "You have to prove it to me, if you dare."

"How?"

Micki eyed him warily, somehow certain she was walking into a trap, yet unable to resist flinging his challenge back at him.

"In no way that's frightening, so stop looking like a startled doe ready to bolt for the bushes." His soft, reasoning tone made her more wary still. She didn't trust him and it showed on her expression. His sigh was elaborately exaggerated. "Simply agree to see me occasionally, talk to me."

"And that's all?" In no way could she keep the blatant surprise from her face. His soft laughter skipped along her nerve endings.

"That's all."

It was too simple. Micki knew it was too simple, yet she had accepted his dare. Momentarily she had a very uneasy feeling she'd been had. Well, so be it, she shrugged mentally. If things got sticky she could always find an excuse for not seeing him. And maybe, just maybe, she could finally banish the pain, consign the memories to oblivion forever. Self-confidence won.

"All right." If she was so sure of herself, why was her voice so whispery? "I must go now," she lied. "I'm expected for dinner."

"Not so fast." His hand came up to catch her chin, lifting her face so he could see her eyes. "When can I see you?"

"I—I don't know." Her tongue stumbled over her words. "I have a lot to do and—"

"Friday," he cut in. "For dinner. I'll pick you up at seven thirty."

"All right, Friday." Micki tried to ignore her sudden leap of anticipation. "I'll be ready."

"Good." His hand dropped to her arm and he moved back, away from the door, drawing her with him. Ignoring her insistence that he needn't walk her to her car, he ushered her through the doorway and along the hall.

The heat hit her like a physical blow when they stepped out of the building. And like some blow to the head it seemed to knock her thinking back onto dead center. Was she out of her mind agreeing to have dinner with him? It sounded innocent enough, but Micki had the sinking sensation that Wolf hadn't had an innocent urge since puberty. She waited until he had opened the car door for her and she had slid onto the seat before glancing up with a hesitant, "Wolf, about Friday."

"What about it?" They were the first words he'd uttered since leaving the apartment and Micki feared the hard sound of his tone.

"Where are we going?" she sighed in defeat. "How should I dress?"

The sardonic curve of his mouth left her in little doubt that he'd been perfectly aware that she'd been about to make a stab at getting out of the date.

"Nothing fancy." Wolf's grin was pure animal. Wolf animal. "We'll take a run down the coast to Wildwood. The restaurant's quiet and the food's good. I hope you like Greek food."

"I do."

Micki turned the key and the motor sprang to life. Wolf closed the door gently but firmly. Knowing there was no possible way out of it now, Micki backed the car around and drove off the lot.

By the time Micki parked her car in the driveway of her father's house she had a nervous stomach and a sick headache. Moving listlessly, she followed the flagstone path to the back door. Before entering, she straightened her spine and composed her features. The scene that met her eyes was so homey and domestic that for a brief moment she felt like an interloper. Regina stood at the kitchen counter grating cheese to top the salad Bruce was tossing in a large wooden bowl.

"Hi, princess, you're just in time for dinner." Her father's warm tone sent the alien feeling packing. "How's Cindy?"

"Blossoming." Micki grinned. Stealing a slim wedge of tomato from the bowl, she added, "I love the house."

"Did she have the fun of surprising you?" Regina turned from the cheese, an uncertain smile on her lips.

"Mmm," Micki nodded, finishing the tomato. "I was properly stunned."

"I'm glad." Regina transferred the grated cheese to the table. "Run into anyone else you know?"

Micki felt her face go stiff. Had her seemingly accidental meeting with Wolf been planned? Could his desire to see her, talk to her, be part of Regina's campaign to cement a friendship between herself and Micki? Micki stared at Regina's mildly inquiring expression as her mind went over those few fantastic minutes she spent in Wolf's apartment. No, she decided firmly. If the meeting had been part of a let's-be-friends play, Wolf would not have made his own play. Her father rescued her from the need to answer Regina's question.

"What's all this about a surprise from Cindy?"

"I didn't know she was pregnant," Micki answered quickly.

"And I inadvertently let the cat out of the bag before Micki left this morning," Regina supplied contritely.

"But all went well." Micki finished the tale dramatically. "Boy, was I surprised."

During the dinner Bruce glanced at Micki and asked, "Are you going with us tonight, honey?"

"Oh, dear, I forgot," Regina moaned, her face stricken. "I was so busy telling Micki something I wasn't supposed to, I failed to tell her what I was supposed to."

Totally confused, Micki begged, "Do you think you

could untangle that for me, Dad? I'm afraid I must have missed something."

"Nothing very earth-shattering," Bruce chuckled. "We've been invited to watch the Night in Venice from the Gallagers' deck. When Dolly and Mike heard you'd be home, they asked me to tell you to come along, as they'd love to see you."

"The Night in Venice," Micki replied faintly. "I—I don't know—I—"

"You don't have other plans, do you?" Her father's face wore a confused question mark.

"No, but," Micki hedged, then offered lamely, "but I don't want to intrude."

"Intrude!" Now his face reflected sheer disbelief. "Dolly and Mike were at your christening. How could you possibly intrude?"

"All right." For the second time in less than two hours, Micki sighed in defeat. "I'd like to come."

It was a bare-faced lie. The last thing Micki wanted was to sit on that particular deck. It was on that deck she had been introduced to one Wolfgang Karl Renninger.

CHAPTER 3

As soon as the dishes were rinsed and stacked in the dishwasher, Micki escaped to her room with a murmured, "I'll be ready," when her father said they would be leaving around eight.

After stripping off her clothes, she headed for the shower. She felt half sick to her stomach and there was a throbbing in her temples that grew stronger with each passing minute. Standing under the tepid spray, water cascading over her head and down her body, Micki decided her acceptance of Wolf's taunting challenge had not been too bright. She knew what he wanted. What he'd always wanted from any woman hapless enough to wander into his orbit. And he thought she'd under persuasion be willing to answer his wants.

About who you're sleeping with.

His words echoed in her mind so clearly she jerked her head around to see if he hadn't somehow slipped into the shower with her. Knowing she was being silly, yet unable to control her reaction, she turned the water off and stepped out of the stall. Raking her memory, she tried to recall his exact tone as well as his words. Once again his words, complete with his shading, came sharp and clear.

Had he sounded derisive? Mocking? Angry? Micki shook her head, she couldn't pinpoint it. The word jealousy leaped into her mind, but with a snort she rejected it. Wolf jealous? Never.

Another thought slithered into her mind and she felt herself go hot then cold. That he'd asked the question in the first place must mean he'd taken for granted that she was sleeping with someone. The vaguely sick feeling in her stomach deepened. She had not denied it. Quite the opposite. The reply she'd flung at him could easily be taken as confirmation.

Her thoughts tormented her as she dressed. Damn him. Whenever she considered herself, her life-style, at all, it was along the lines of independent, self-sufficient, and confident. In less than one hour Wolf had managed to undermine her self-image. Suddenly she felt vulnerable, confused, and much younger than her twenty-five years. Damn him. Her last thoughts before leaving her room were *He's going to give me trouble, I know it, and I don't know what to do about it.*

They walked to the bay, enjoying the sweetness of the early evening ocean breeze. The Gallager house was full of people, as it always was the evening of Night in Venice. As it was still early, most of the people were milling about, laughing, talking, helping themselves to the large array of snacks Dolly had set out.

Micki had always enjoyed the Gallagers' company. About her father's age, they were a warm, friendly couple who liked having people around. When she was a little girl, Micki had loved visiting them.

After exchanging greetings and hugs and a few moments of small talk, Micki wandered out onto the nearly empty deck. She knew that before too long both the deck she was on and the one above her would be crowded with people, but for now, for just a few minutes, she could savor the near solitude.

As she crossed the deck toward the railing, Micki

glanced around. As far as she could see on either side, on the docks at street endings, on the porches and wide decks of apartment houses and private homes, people were gathered for the once-a-year show.

Making her way to a chair placed in a corner of the deck, Micki gazed out over the bay, affected, as she'd always been, by the molten gold sheen cast on the water by the fiery ball of westering sun.

She sat down and looked around idly, then froze in the chair, her hands gripping the armrests. Closing her eyes, she stifled a groan against the memory that would no longer stay locked away.

She had been sitting very near this spot when she'd first seen him. He had had one broad shoulder propped against a support beam and was half sitting on the rail when she'd felt his eyes on her and glanced up. She'd frozen then too, held fast to the chair by the bold stare from his silvery eyes. Micki experienced again the breathlessness she'd felt that night, the sensation that although six feet of deck separated them he was actually touching her. The shortness of breath had lasted until Mike had strolled up to talk to him and drew his eyes away from her.

Micki had studied his profile covertly while the two men talked. In his late twenties or early thirties, she'd judged, and was, without question, the most sexy, exciting-looking male she'd ever seen.

She'd been positive her heart had stopped when at Mike's quick, smiling nod, he'd lazily pushed himself away from the rail and followed Mike over the deck to her.

She had been amused at his name when Mike made the introductions and she'd made no attempt to hide it when she raised her eyes to his.

"Wolfgang?" she'd repeated in a laughing tone.

"Pitiful, isn't it?" he'd drawled. "It's a traditional name in my family. I, unfortunately, got tagged with it, being the firstborn male child." His eyes seemed to absorb her as he added, "Call me Wolf."

45

"And *are* you?" Micki had been amazed at the insolent sound of her voice. "A wolf, I mean."

"Of course," he'd returned smoothly, a wicked grin flashing on his tan face. "Isn't everyone who is single and unattached on the prowl?" He'd cocked his head to one side and those bold, silver eyes roamed over her, from head to foot to head again. "If you weren't so young, I may have decided to stalk you." His eyes laughed at the sudden pinkness in her face. His voice dropped to a low caress. "I still might."

Struck speechless, Micki had stared at him, praying for some bright, crushing words to pop into her head. None did, and then it didn't matter, for someone—that throaty voice could only have belonged to Regina—inside called to him and he turned away from her. He took one step, then glanced back at her, the wicked grin flashing again.

"A pleasure meeting you"—he paused—"young Micki."

Micki had gone all hot and flushed, first with embarrassment, then with anger. *He spoke to me as if I was a little girl,* she'd thought furiously, *and I'm not. I'm nineteen, for heaven's sake and I hope I never see that bigheaded, overbearing Wolf again.*

Even so, her anger and hope notwithstanding, his image filled her mind the rest of the night and she saw very little of the evening's entertainment.

"Well, honey, I see you've found a good seat for the show."

Micki blinked away the past and glanced up at her father, a shaky smile on her lips.

"Yes," she answered vaguely, noticing, for the first time, that it was nearly dark. "Shouldn't it be getting under way soon?"

"How far away were you?" Bruce laughed. "If you'll merely look to your right, you'll see it's nearly on top of us."

Micki's eyes followed the direction of his casually

46

waved hand. Then she whispered a surprised, "Oh!" Sure enough, the procession of gaily decorated, brightly lighted boats of all sizes was indeed nearly on top of them.

For several minutes Micki watched the parade of boats, enjoying the reflection of the lights on the water, laughing at the clowning antics of the men in the smaller boats, and waving at the people of all ages aboard the cleverly festooned crafts.

But her eyes soon drifted to that one spot at the rail, clouding over with the rush of memories.

She had not seen him again for almost a week. Then, when she was finally beginning to get his image out of her mind, she felt the touch of his silvery eyes again. At the time she'd thought it was very strange. She'd been walking near the far end of the boardwalk with Cindy and two other girls, all of them laughing as they munched on slices of pizza, when she felt an eerie shiver skip down her spine. What had made her lift her head, glance around, she didn't know, but she'd just felt compelled to look. This time he was propped against the boardwalk's pipelike railing, his eyes fastened on her. He didn't call to her or even wave, but the grin flashed white and wicked and his eyes seemed to speak of things beyond her wildest imaginings. She had caught herself just in time from choking on her pizza and had hurried on, but after a dozen steps she'd glanced back to find his eyes still on her.

Early in August she'd seen him again. That time she'd been leaving the theater after the early evening showing of a controversial R-rated movie. She had been with her gang and the comments, both pro and con on the film, were flying hot and heavy. Wolf, with a beautiful, high-fashion-type redhead clinging to his arm, was going in to the late evening showing. Micki nearly bumped into him. There was no grin this time, but as he passed her one eyelid came down in a slow, suggestive wink.

And then, in late August, there was a cookout at a

friend's beachfront house and all the unbelievable events that followed it.

There must have been twenty of them, not counting her friend's parents and the people they'd invited. After they'd eaten, they'd split up into two-man teams for a sand-sculpting contest, which, the adults vowed, they'd judge impartially. Micki had been teamed with Tony Menella, and even with all the horseplay and general craziness, their sculpture of a reclining nude had won hands down.

As twilight settled gently on the beach, Cindy had suggested they go hunting in the sand. They'd started out as a group, but their ranks thinned as some quit to go back to the house and others roamed farther along the beach.

Toting a brown bag to hold her dubious treasures, Micki found herself alone with a boy she'd met that night for the first time. Searching her mind, she came up with the name David Bender. She crossed her fingers in hope it was the right one.

"What happened to all the other kids?" Micki's fingers twined behind her back. "David?"

"Beats me." He glanced around scanning the beach. "I guess most of them got bored." His still boyishly slim shoulders lifted in a shrug. "Did you find anything worth keeping?"

"No." Micki laughed.

"Me either." David laughed with her. "Want to sit and rest awhile before heading back?" He shot her a shy look. "We've come down the beach pretty far."

"Okay," Micki answered flippantly, plopping down at the base of a low sand dune. "You're from up near Margate, aren't you?" she asked after he'd dropped onto the sand less than a foot away from her.

"Yeah," David nodded, not looking at her, his eyes fixed on the darkening ocean.

Sighing softly, Micki leaned back against the gentle slope of the dune, her eyes studying him with mild interest. About her own age, she thought, maybe even a little younger. He still had the look of the high-school boy, she mused from the exalted distance of one completed year of college. Unbidden, a picture of Wolfgang Renninger rose in her mind. Micki had to compress her lips to keep from laughing out loud at the comparison. Unfair, she chided herself sternly. Wolf's a mature man, while David's still in the throes of adolescence. She should have remembered how hot the blood can flow in teenaged boys.

"You're a very pretty girl." David's voice came softly close to her ear. During her perusal of him, he'd settled back into the dune, turned onto his side to face her. "Are you going steady with anyone?"

Startled out of her contemplation, Micki turned her head to find his face close to hers. Surprised, she smiled nervously. "No, not steady. I'm too busy with college and—David, what—?"

His soft, moist lips silenced her. With an inward sigh, Micki lay perfectly still, his inexperienced kiss drawing no response from her. It was a mistake. Her lack of interest seemed to spur a determination in him to make her feel something. The pressure on her lips increased painfully. Suddenly his hands pushed her beach wrap open, tore at the skimpy top of her bikini as his body rolled on top of her.

Her first reaction was sharp anger. Who did this jerk think he was, pawing at her? Bringing her hands up, she pushed at his shoulders, fully expecting him to move off her at once and apologize sheepishly. Fear began when she couldn't dislodge him. He was a lot stronger than he looked. With all her twisting and turning she could not escape his lips. She couldn't breathe and she felt sure that if he didn't lift his head soon she'd faint from lack of air. Panic shot through her when his fingers dug into her now-exposed breasts and one bony knee attempted to pry her legs apart. This couldn't be happening. Not to her.

Blackness was stealing into her mind when his lips slid

from hers, moved to fasten, hurtfully, on the soft skin on the side of her neck.

"David, stop," Micki gasped between huge gulps of consciousness-saving breaths. Fear lent inspiration as, struggling frantically, she lied. "I've got to get back, my father will be coming to pick me up."

"You don't have to go anywhere," David panted, his fingers digging viciously into her breasts. "I heard you tell Cindy you'd be alone all weekend because your folks are out of town."

His lips moved in a sucking action, drawing a cry of pain from her. Nausea filled her throat when his knee succeeded in pushing her legs apart and his slender frame pressed her deeper into the gritty sand.

"David, please stop." She was crying openly, her sobs catching at her throat when she felt his hand move down her body, tug at her bikini bottom. "No!" Her voice rose in a muffled scream of pure desperation.

"Hey!" David yelped loudly, then suddenly his weight was removed, yanked away from her violently.

"You stupid crumb." The enraged, unfamiliar growl was followed by the stinging sound of a hard, open-handed blow and a loud cry of pain from David. "Get the hell out of here or I'll break you in half."

Still crying, blinking against the tears that blurred her vision, Micki cringed back when big hands grasped her shoulders, lifted her from the sand.

"It's all right, youngster, he's gone." The soft tone that had replaced the enraged growl was recognizable now as belonging to Wolf Renninger.

"He—he—he tried to—"

"I know," Wolf snapped, preventing her from saying the word *rape*. "But it's over now." He went on in a softer tone. He pulled her impersonally, protectively against his broad, hard chest, brushed the sand from her back with his big hand. "I'll see that you get home safely."

50

"Oh, no," Micki moaned, rubbing her forehead back and forth over the smooth material of his shirt.

"No?" Wolf repeated impatiently. "What do you mean, no?"

"You don't understand," she wailed. "Dad and Regina are away for the weekend. I'll be alone in the house and David knows it. What if he—?" Micki paused to swallow a fresh lump of fear. "I don't want to go home."

He cursed softly, then was very still for long seconds before, moving away from her, he said decisively, "Okay, you can come with me for a while, then I'm taking you home."

The harshness of his voice confused and frightened her. Meekly, after hurriedly tugging her suit top into place and fastening her beach coat at the neck, she followed in his wake as he walked around the sand dune and strode toward the road where a low-slung car was parked.

"Come on," Wolf gritted irritably at her slow progress through the tall grass.

As she slid onto the seat of the sports car, Micki slanted a quick look at him through her long lashes, wondering what she'd said, or done, to make him so angry. Surely he didn't think she had encouraged David in any way? She jumped when the door slammed beside her, and again when his own slammed, after he'd folded his long frame onto the seat behind the wheel. Opening her mouth to ask him what was wrong, Micki glanced at him and closed her lips quickly at the hard, rigid set of his face. Wolf started the car and made a U-turn on Ocean Drive, heading away from the city.

"Where are we going?" Micki asked hesitantly.

"I've got my boat docked not far from here," he replied tersely. "I have to move it."

They drove a short distance beyond the city limits, then Wolf turned off the drive toward the bay where he parked the car on a small lot in front of a rather rundown building with a red neon sign that read BAR & GRILL.

51

"Where were you?"

The question was punctuated by his hard tug on the hand brake. For a second Micki blinked at him in confusion, then his meaning registered.

"At a cookout beach party, at a friend's home."

"Did you go dressed like that?" he snapped.

"No, of course not," Micki snapped back, beginning to feel a little steadier as the shock from her experience receded. "My clothes are at the house."

"What's this friend's name and phone number?"

"You're not going to call her?" Micki cried.

"Yes, I am," Wolf sighed in exasperation. "When you don't come back they're liable to call the police. If they haven't already."

Micki hadn't thought of the furor her absence might cause. Chastised, she murmured the name and number.

"Okay, I've got it." He opened the car door and stepped out. "Stay here, I'll be back in a minute."

The door swung closed with a loud bang. Biting her lip, Micki wondered again why he was so angry. As the minute stretched into five and then ten, Micki's temper flared. What was he doing all this time? Probably having a drink with the boys, while she sat alone in a dark parking lot. And who did he think he was anyway? He had no right to snap and snarl at her like some untamed beast of the wild. By the time he returned, she talked herself into a fury.

"What were you doing all this time?" she demanded the minute he'd opened the door beside her. "Making time with the barmaid?"

"Don't take that tone with me, youngster." Wolf's soft voice held a definite warning. "What I do, who I make time with, is no concern of yours. If you've got any sense at all, you'll guard that nasty little tongue. You couldn't even handle Joe College back there. I'd crush you like an annoying little gnat. Now get out of the car, I'm taking you home."

52

"But—" she began.

"Out," he cut in harshly.

Micki bit her lip, feeling very young, and very inexperienced, and very, very stupid. He was right, of course, she had no right to question him. If it hadn't been for him . . . She shuddered. Belatedly she remembered she hadn't even thanked him. No wonder he was angry. Knowing what she had to do, she drew a deep breath, slid off the seat, and stood before him, her head bent.

"I'm—I'm sorry, Mr. Renninger," she whispered contritely. "I know you must think I'm a stupid little ingrate." Wetting her dry lips, Micki lifted her head to look at him, her eyes made even brighter by the shimmer of tears. "I—I haven't even thanked you for helping me. But I am grateful, truly, and—and—" She had to pause to swallow against the tightness in her throat. "I wanted you to know I didn't invite that attack."

"I didn't think you had." Wolf's much gentler tone brought a fresh rush of tears to her eyes. "Don't cry, young Micki." His hand came up to cradle her face, one long finger brushed at her tears. "I know it was a bad experience, but you're unhurt and—" He broke off and leaned toward her. "He didn't hurt you, did he?"

"No, not really." Micki shook her head, drawing a deep breath to combat the increase in heartbeat his nearness caused. "The only thing hurt is my dignity."

"It will heal," he murmured, lowering his head closer to hers. His fingers shook as if he'd had a sudden chill, then he snatched his hand away as though her skin had burned him. "Come on, kid, I've got to get you home." The gentleness had gone, replaced by an edgy roughness Micki didn't understand, as she didn't understand the hard emphasis he'd placed on the word *kid*.

"But what about your car?"

"It isn't mine. It belongs to the guy that owns this place."

Grasping her arm, he hurried her around the building

and onto a rickety pier. Secured to the pier, bathed dimly in the glow from the building's side windows, was a cabin cruiser that brought a small gasp from Micki.

"Is that beautiful thing yours?" she asked in an awed tone.

"Yes," Wolf replied shortly. "Go aboard, I want to cast off."

"Please." Micki's hand caught his arm as he turned away. "Could I have a quick tour of her before we go?"

The muscles in his arm tensed under her fingers and Micki was sure he was about to refuse. Then with a soft sigh of resignation, he said crisply, "All right, a very quick tour."

He helped her to board the shadowy craft, then, one hand at her waist to guide her, he led her across the deck and down a short flight of stairs with a murmured, "Careful." There was the sound of a switch being flicked and Micki blinked against the sudden light that filled the small salon she was standing in. Glancing around at the sparse, masculine furnishings, she breathed, "How many does she sleep?"

"Ten," Wolf replied curtly, indicating a narrow portal across the room. Micki stepped through the portal into an equally narrow passageway, which had two doors on each side. When she hesitated at the first door on her left, Wolf grated, "Get on with it."

Biting back the retort that sprang to her lips, Micki pushed the door open. The cabin contained a small fitted dresser and four fitted bunks. The cabin next to it was exactly the same. As she withdrew from the second cabin, Wolf opened the door directly across the passage, with a terse, "The head."

The small, but adequate-sized bathroom was equipped with a stainless steel toilet, shower stall, and fitted washbowl. Wolf was standing at the open door of the last cabin when she emerged from the head. He made a half bow as she approached him. "The captain's quarters," he drawled mockingly.

Feeling herself grow warm under his mocking glance, Micki unfastened her beach coat and preceded him into the cabin. It was larger than the other two cabins. Instead of fitted bunks it contained a built-in bed, not quite as wide as a regular double bed.

At sight of the bed, Micki's body was suddenly suffused with warmth. Feeling constricted, she pulled her beach coat open. Casting about in her mind for something to say to the silent man standing just inside the cabin, she turned slowly.

"Is—is this where you sle—" The words died on her lips at the sudden, fierce look on his face. Her breathing stopped as he walked to her, his silvery eyes gleaming dangerously behind narrowed lids.

"What's wrong?" she gasped, terrified by the look of him.

"That creep bastard marked you," he snarled softly, bending over her to examine her throat and the smooth skin below her shoulders.

"Oh, no," she groaned, her hand flying to her neck. "Is it very bad?"

"Bad enough," he clipped, straightening. "Sit down, I'll get some antiseptic to put on it."

Disregarding his order, she walked to the small mirror above the dresser and leaned toward it to peer closely at the red marks.

"I told you to sit." The hard sound of his voice set her teeth on edge.

"I'm not a dog," Micki flared, close to tears.

"You're telling me," he drawled, holding his hand out to her. "Come on, infant, let me dab this stuff on you."

Ignoring his hand, Micki walked by him stiffly, miffed at the term *infant*. Sitting down gingerly on the very edge of the bed, she lifted her head to expose her neck, and closed her eyes. When the antiseptic touched the abrasion,

55

she drew her breath in sharply and shut her eyes more tightly to stem the corresponding sting in her eyes.

"Sorry," he muttered softly. He was so close, his warm breath feathered her skin, setting off a clamoring inside her that ended in a visible shiver. "I could beat him up for doing this to you." The soft intensity of his tone increased her shivering. Keeping her eyes tightly closed, holding her breath, Micki sat immobile. Something strange was happening to her. Something strange, and a little scary, and almost unbearably exciting.

The feather light touch of his lips on her skin felt like a touch from an exposed electrical wire. Trembling, Micki moaned deep in her throat. She heard his raspy, indrawn breath an instant before he sighed softly, groaned, "Dear God, Micki."

His mouth touched hers gently, experimentally. When she didn't flinch away, the pressure increased and his hands grasped her upper arms. Her heart beating wildly, Micki returned the kiss. She gasped against his mouth when the hard tip of his tongue moved slowly across her lips, but she obeyed the silent command to part them. His mouth still gentle, exploring, he straightened, drawing her to her feet in front of him.

Micki didn't know what was happening to her. She had been kissed before, many times, but never had she felt this sweet joy zinging through her veins, this light-headed, intoxicating sensation. When she swayed toward him, touched his body with her own, he lifted his head, held her away from him.

"I've got to take you home," he rasped unevenly.

"Why?" Micki asked huskily.

"Don't you know?" Wolf groaned. "Have you really no idea of the effect you're having on me?"

Elation shot through her, gave her the courage to lean toward him, slide the tip of her tongue across his mouth. He went stone still, then gritted. "Where the hell did you learn that trick?"

Micki's eyes went wide at his rough tone. "From you, just now. I've never—never—"

"Why did you do it?" His growl had lost its bite.

"Because"—Micki wet her lips, felt a curl of excitement when his eyes dropped to her mouth—"because I was afraid you weren't going to kiss me again—and I wanted you to."

"You're too young to know what you want." Micki's head was shaking a denial before he'd finished speaking, but he didn't give her time to voice it. "If I kissed you, I mean really kissed you, you'd be fighting me in a cold panic within seconds, exactly like you were fighting that teenage Don Juan back at the beach."

"No, I wouldn't," Micki denied softly. "I didn't want him to kiss me. I do want you to."

His silvery eyes stared hard into hers, then dropped to her mouth, then lifted to her eyes again. "I must be out of my mind," he muttered. "I never should have brought you here after the jealousy I felt of that punk."

"You felt jealous of David!" Micki exclaimed. "But why?"

"Because"—Wolf's voice was very low as he drew her slowly against his long frame—"I wanted to be in exactly the same position he was in, you beautiful fool."

This time there was very little gentleness. His lips crushed hers, forcing them apart roughly. His tongue probed hungrily. Flaring lights actually seemed to explode behind her eyes. Raising her arms, she curled them around his neck, needing suddenly to be closer to him. He half groaned, half growled into her mouth, then his hands moved across her shoulders, down her back, molding her to his hard body. Responding to the demands of her body, Micki arched her hips against him. At once lips pulled away from hers, moved in a fiery path over her cheek to her ear.

"Micki, stop me while you still can." His voice held half plea, half command.

"I don't want you to stop." The moment the words were out she knew she spoke the truth. She had never behaved like this before in her life, yet she knew she wanted to, had to, belong to this man.

Although his hands still held her tightly to him, he lifted his head, gave her another of those hard stares. "You've been with a man before?"

Micki hesitated, knowing somehow that if she told him the truth he'd put her from him, take her home. Praying that in the dim light her flush would look like guilt, she lowered her lashes, whispered, "Yes."

A flash of something—pain, disgust—twisted his face. He gave an almost imperceptible shake of his head, then lowered his mouth to within a whisper of hers. Again she heard that half groan, half growl.

"I don't care." His hands spread over her hips, pulling her tightly against him. "Oh, God, baby, I want you."

Her beach coat and her bikini were removed gently but swiftly. For the first time in her life Micki stood naked before a man, amazed that she felt no shame or fear. As he undressed, his eyes, gleaming like liquid silver, moved slowly over her body, the burning, naked hunger in them igniting an eagerness in her to be in his arms, be part of him.

Slowly, expertly, his mouth and hands an exquisite torture, he fanned the flame inside her to a roaring blaze. Gasping, moaning softly deep in her throat, her lips leaving tiny, urgent kisses on his neck, his shoulders, she welcomed him when, finally, his body covered hers. Moments later he cursed her.

"Damn you!" Wolf's tone held anger, but an odd note of satisfaction as well. "You lied to me."

"Yes," she admitted into the curve of his shoulder, her arms tightening around his waist, refusing to let go.

"Oh, baby, baby." He kissed her mouth tenderly. "I'm sorry."

58

"I'm not," Micki replied honestly. "I wanted this as badly as you did, Wolf."

"Sweet Lord, I've found myself a sexy teenage vixen," Wolf muttered huskily, his body moving excitingly.

"You'd better enjoy it while you can," Micki laughed teasingly. "I'll only be a teenager two more months."

"A vixen and a tease," Wolf moaned between short, quick breaths, then, "Oh, God, honey, kiss me."

Micki's initiation into the world of serious lovemaking lasted until three o'clock the following morning. Wolf was a master tutor, and under his ardent guidance she caught a glimpse of the wondrous things his eyes had seemed to speak of that time on the boardwalk. Exhausted, she curled still closer to him, heard him laugh softly as his arms tightened around her.

"That was just the first chapter of the text," he teased. "Do you think you'll graduate?"

"Cum laude," she murmured sleepily and was rewarded by a light kiss on the corner of her mouth.

"Go to sleep, honey," Wolf whispered into her ear.

CHAPTER 4

"Wake up, honey."

Micki jumped at the sound of her father's quiet voice, the gentle touch of his hand on her arm.

"Is it over?"

Sitting up straight, she winced at the twinge of pain at the base of her spine and brought her hand up to massage the stiffness in her neck caused by the hard rim of the aluminum chair. Glancing around, she saw the deck was empty of all the other people. What time was it?

"Over an hour ago." Bruce laughed softly. "The party's breaking up. It's time to go home."

"I'm ready."

Moving carefully, Micki lifted her cramped body out of the chair, one hand going to her mouth to cover a wide yawn. In a young-girl, sleepy voice, she apologized, thanked, and said good night to her indulgently smiling host and hostess, then followed her father and Regina out to the hushed sidewalk.

Trailing a few steps behind the couple, she watched as her father's arm slid around his wife's waist, heard his low voice murmur something close to her ear. Regina apparently disagreed with what her father had said, for her head moved slowly in a negative shake. The argument, if that's what it was, was obviously not over anything very serious. With a sigh of relief, Micki heard Regina laugh softly.

Dropping a few steps farther behind in order to give them complete privacy, Micki's fingers curled tightly into the palm of her hand. Well, she'd missed it again. It had been six years since she'd gone to watch the Night in Venice and she'd seen practically none of it. And for exactly the same reason—thoughts of Wolf had absorbed her attention, her senses.

Angrily rejecting the image of him that rose in her mind, Micki centered her thoughts on the couple a few feet ahead of her, wondering if she could be the bone of contention between them. She hoped not, but had the sinking sensation that she was. For all Regina's declared wish that they be friends, Micki was still very unsure of her. Their past relationship had been fraught with so much jealousy, so much resentment, that Micki was unconvinced of the permanency of their truce.

The minute Micki entered the house, Bruce ended her conjecturing.

"There is only one way to find out," he stated in a tone of amused exasperation. "And that's ask her."

"Bruce, please," Regina pleaded softly. "Not tonight, she's tired and—"

"She's wide awake now," Bruce insisted, studying his daughter closely. "Princess, I'm going to ask you something and I want you to answer honestly. Will you?"

"Yes, of course." Micki's gaze flew from her father's laughing eyes to Regina's worried ones. What was this all about? Her father answered her silent question.

"I want to take Regina on a second honeymoon," he said quietly, his suddenly serious, love-filled eyes resting on his wife's face.

"And?" Micki prompted, confused as to what a proposed second honeymoon had to do with her.

"Regina insists that it would be selfish of us to go away at this time."

"Selfish?" Micki repeated blankly. "I don't understand. In what way would it be selfish?"

A satisfied grin spread over her father's face. "You see?" he asked Regina before turning back to Micki. "Regina is afraid you'll feel, well, deserted, if we went away so soon after your return home."

"But that's ridiculous!" Micki cried. "When were you thinking of going?"

"Not till the end of the month." Bruce's eyes filled with pride and tenderness as he studied Micki's face. "It will take me until then to tie up some loose ends at the office."

Micki looked directly at Regina. "By the end of the month I expect the majority of my time will be spent in learning my new job." Her eyes swung back to her father. "I think a second honeymoon is a lovely idea, especially as I don't remember your ever having a first."

"It was impossible for me to leave the office at that time," Bruce defended himself. "And since then the time just didn't seem right." Bruce paused, then went on softly. "With one thing and another."

"Well, then," Micki spoke quickly, knowing too well that she was the one thing and Regina's behavior the other. "If you feel the time is now right, then go, and don't worry about me. I'm a big girl now and quite used to taking care of myself." At the contrite expression that crossed her father's face at her last words, Micki willed a sparkle into her eyes and shaded her voice with teasing excitement. "Where were you thinking of going, or is that a secret?"

"No secret." Micki felt relief rush through her at the way her father's face lit up. "I had thought San Francisco, I've always wanted to see it." His voice grew eager. "We could rent a car, drive through the Redwoods, along the coast, Carmel, Big Sur."

Watching Regina's face, Micki could see her father's

eagerness reflected there. Although she had been arguing against the trip, it was obvious Regina wanted to go.

"Sounds super." Micki spoke directly to Regina. "So do it. Make your arrangements and take off. I promise you I will be fine."

Grabbing Regina up in a bear hug, Bruce spun her around, laughing. "What did I tell you, darling? Is my girl something special or not?"

"Very special." Regina spoke for the first time. When he turned back to Micki, Regina mouthed a silent thank you at her.

Wide awake now, Micki murmured, "I think I'll sit on the porch a few minutes," when her father and Regina moved toward the stairs. "You two go on up, I'll lock up."

Micki stepped out onto the porch, then turned back to get a sweater from the hall closet. A mist rolling in off the ocean had turned the air cool and clammy. Settling back on the porch lounger, she watched the mist swirl and thicken, turn the light from the street lamp into an eerie orangish glow.

The mist had been like this that morning.

Shifting irritably on the thickly padded cushion, Micki tried to push the thought away. She didn't want to think about it. Didn't want to remember. Her shifting, her silent protests, were in vain. The floodgate of memory, which had sprung a leak earlier, now burst completely, swamping her, carrying her helplessly back through time.

Micki stirred when the warmth of Wolf's body was removed from hers. Through eyelids heavy with sleep, she watched him, his form barely discernible in the gray, pre-dawn half light. Moving noiselessly, he stepped into his jeans, fastened them, then pulled a battered sweat shirt over his head. Fear shot through her as he moved across the floor to the door.

"Wolf?" Micki's voice betrayed her fear. "Where are you going?"

64

At the sound of his name Wolf turned, the fear in her tone brought him back to the bed in a few long strides. Bending, he dropped a soft kiss on her lips.

"I have to move the boat," he explained quietly, one long finger outlining her mouth. "Go back to sleep. As soon as I have her docked at the marina I'll come back to bed." His lips touched hers again, lingered, then he was moving across the cabin, out the door.

Micki closed her eyes tightly, but it was no good; she couldn't sleep with him gone. Slipping out of the bed, and a moment later out of the cabin, she hurried into the tiny bathroom. She was stepping under the shower spray when she heard the boat's engine flare into life. Bracing herself with one hand, she washed her body with the other while Wolf backed the boat away from the pier and swung it around. When the craft was relatively steady, she stepped out of the shower stall, grabbed for the towel, probably Wolf's, that hung on a small fitted bar, and rubbed herself down briskly.

Back in the cabin, she stretched languorously. The tautening of her breasts brought the remembered feel of Wolf's hands, and her nipples set into diamond-hard points. Oh, Wolf. Just to think his name sent her blood racing through her veins, set her pulses hammering out of control. She couldn't wait until he'd docked the boat, she had to see him now.

Glancing around, she grimaced as her eyes settled on her bikini and beach coat, laying in an untidy heap where Wolf had tossed them. Shaking her head in rejection of the beachwear, she went to the cabin's one small closet and rummaged through shirts and jackets—obviously too short to cover the bare necessities—until her hand clutched and withdrew a bright yellow rain slicker. Pulling it on hastily, uncaring how incongruous she looked, she left the cabin, fastening the buckle closings as she went.

Not once did she pause to ask herself why she was

where she was, with a man she knew practically nothing about. Not once did she wonder about how suddenly it had happened. She was there. It had happened. Never before had she felt so tinglingly alive, so totally happy. But she didn't even pause to think of that. The only thought that filled her mind was that she had to be near him, see him. The whys and how of it would torment her later.

When she stepped onto the deck she came to an abrupt halt, her hand groping for something solid to steady herself with. An off-white mist lay over everything, muffling sound, obscuring visibility. The deck was beaded and slick with moisture. Placing her bare feet carefully, Micki moved cautiously toward the canopied section that housed the wheel, and the man who stood at that wheel, alert tenseness in every line of his tall, muscular frame.

She thought her progress was silent, yet the moment she stepped under the canopy, his left arm was extended backward.

"Come stand by me." Wolf's hushed tone blended with the cotton blanket that surrounded the boat.

Without a word Micki moved to his side, sighed with contentment when his arm closed around her, drew her close to his hard strength.

"Why didn't you go back to sleep?" Still the same hushed tone, not scolding, a simple question. He did not look at her, and her eyes following the direction of his intent gaze, she answered as simply.

"I wanted to be with you."

She saw his hand tighten on the wheel at the same instant the muscles in his arm tautened. He slanted her a quick glance and an amused smile curved his firmly etched mouth.

"I see you've made free with my shower and bath soap." The smile deepened. "Bedecked yourself with the latest yachting creations from Paris also."

"But of course," Micki teased back. "This particular

number was labeled MORNING SUNLIGHT THROUGH HEAVY GAUZE CURTAINS. Does my lord approve?"

Wolf's soft laughter was an exciting, provocative attack on her senses.

"But of course," he mimicked her seriously. "Still, I think I prefer the, er, more basic ensemble you were wearing earlier."

Flushed with pleasure, Micki rubbed her warm cheek against his cool, mist-dampened sweat shirt. Misunderstanding her action and the pink glow on her face, he chided her softly.

"You're a beautiful woman, babe." Wolf's soft tone brooked no argument. "Every soft, satiny inch of you. There's no reason for embarrassment." He paused, then slanted another, harder look at her. "Do you feel shame?"

"No!" Micki's denial was fast, emphatic. "Or embarrassment either." Rising on tiptoe, she placed her lips on the strong column of his throat. "I'm—I'm pleased that you find me attractive."

"Attractive?" Micki could feel the tension ease out of him. "I don't think that adjective quite makes it." Leaning forward, he peered, narrow-eyed, through the moisture-beaded window. "If I ever get this damned boat docked I'll try to come up with the right one. Now be still and let me get on with it."

Micki obeyed him explicably. Barely breathing, she watched as he inched the craft along through the mist-shrouded water, and sighed with relief when he murmured, "There's the marina." When he removed his arm, she stepped back ready to follow any order he might issue.

"Have you ever driven a boat?" Wolf asked tersely as he backed the vessel into the slip.

"Yes," Micki answered quietly, then qualified, "But never one this large."

"Good enough." Their voyage through the mist completed safely, all his intent tenseness fled. His silvery eyes glittered teasingly. "You hold her down and I'll tie her up."

Suiting action to words, he drew her to the wheel, gave a few brief instructions, and then he was gone, swallowed up in the gray-white mist. A moment later she heard the dull thud as the securing line landed on the pier, and then another as he followed it.

When the craft was secured, its engine silent, Wolf slid his arms around the bulky slicker at her waist and held her loosely.

"You hungry, baby?" His low tone, the way his eyes caressed her face, drove all thoughts but one from her mind. "Do you want some breakfast?"

Micki was shaking her head before he finished speaking. Not even trying to mask her feelings, she gazed up at him, her eyes honest and direct.

"I want to go back to bed."

"Good Lord," he breathed huskily, his arms drawing her closer. "What did I ever do to earn you as a reward?"

Pleasure radiated through her entire body at the warmth of his tone, the emotion-darkened gray of his eyes. Her arms, made clumsy by the too-large raincoat, encircled his neck to draw his head closer to hers. A shiver of anticipation skipped down her spine as his hands slid slowly over the smooth, stiff material of the garment.

"Are you wearing anything at all under that slicker?" His face was so near, his cool breath fanned her lips.

Mesmerized by the shiny, tautened skin of his mist-dampened cheeks and the motion of his mouth, Micki whispered a bemused, "No."

His parted lips touched hers in a brief kiss before she felt her lower lip caught inside his mouth, felt his teeth nibble gently on the tender, sensitive skin. Moaning softly, she flicked his teeth with her tongue. Instantly his arms tightened, crushing her against his hard body, and his lips pushed hers apart to receive his hungry, demanding mouth.

Awareness of him sang through every particle of her being. Squirming inside the stiff, confining coat, she strained her body to his, thrilled to the feeling of his body straining to hers.

"Wolf, Wolf." The words filled her mind, whispered past her lips to fill his mouth.

Lifting his head, he stared deeply into her eyes, his own eyes now nearly black with desire. His gaze dropped to her mouth.

"Why are we standing here?" His murmured groan held near pain. One arm clasped firmly around her waist, he led her along the slippery deck, down the steps, and into his cabin. Releasing her, his hands moved to the buckles on the coat.

"I swear, if I don't soon feel the silkiness of you against my skin, I think I'll burst into flames."

And in a sense he did, engulfing her in the conflagration.

They didn't leave the boat all that day or night. In fact they hardly set foot out of his cabin, except when hunger drove them to the tiny galley for sustenance.

At those times they worked together, mostly getting in each other's way. Micki, clad in her mid-thigh-length beach coat, juggled a frying pan around Wolf's large frame as she endeavored to prepare a cheese omelet on the small two-burner cooking unit. Wolf, wearing a belted, knee-length velour robe, stretched long arms around and in front of her in his effort to make a pot of coffee and open a jar of olives.

When Micki opined that had they followed the simple method of flipping a coin to determine who would get the meal the job would have been completed a lot faster, Wolf retorted that it would also have been one hell of a lot less fun.

They went through the same bumping into and laughing procedure while preparing a canned soup and canned corned beef sandwich supper, washed down with canned beer.

And both times, after appeasing the hunger of their stomachs, they went back to the appeasement of their seemingly insatiable hunger for each other.

They slept for short periods when exhaustion could no longer be held at bay, waking every time to come eagerly together, resentful of the hours of separation the need for sleep had imposed.

At one of those times, late in the night, Micki woke first and lay quietly, unmoving beside Wolf's sleeping form. Touching him with her eyes only, she studied him minutely, imprinting his likeness on her mind, in her soul.

Although by now she knew him fully in a physical sense, he was still a stranger. A stranger she was deeply, unconditionally in love with. It was a sobering thought. Sobering and somewhat frightening, for although he had murmured countless, impassioned, exciting love words to her, none had been words of love for her. But then, she had not spoken of her love for him either. Maybe it was all too new, too sudden for both of them. And maybe, she thought with a sageness beyond her years, the avowals of love now would ring false, take on the shadings of an excuse for their wild coming together. Micki shrugged mentally. It didn't matter. She'd face the reality of it all tomorrow. For right now, she knew she loved him, would probably always love him.

Micki's eyes misted over as she stared at his face. He had made her so unbelievably, joyously happy. She loved her father dearly, yet she knew that should Wolf ask her, she would go with him anywhere in the world with never a backward glance. She had had no promises of undying love, had had no solemn words spoken over her, still she felt like a bride on her honeymoon. And no girl's honeymoon, she was certain, had ever been more idyllic, more perfect than this one.

"Why are you crying?" Wolf's tone, though soft, held hard concern.

Blinking against the moisture, Micki snuggled close to him.

"Because I'm happy," she whispered, her lips brushing his taut jaw. "Haven't you ever heard that females cry when they're happy?"

"Yes, I had heard that." The movement of his lips at her temple sent tiny shivers down the back of her neck. "In fact there have been several occasions when I have been the recipient of those happy tears." The admission was made tonelessly, without conceit. "But never for so little."

"Little?" Tilting her head back, Micki looked up at him, her eyes reflecting her confusion. "I don't understand. What do you mean—for so little?"

Lifting his head, he studied her expression, as if trying to determine if her confusion was authentic. Obviously deciding it was, he shook his head in wonder. "Always before, the tears were in response to a gift from me." Wolf's eyes held hers steadily, gauging her reaction. "Jewelry, flowers, things like that," he shrugged, "but always a tangible, usually expensive, object."

Micki gazed back at him, trying, but failing, to keep the hurt from her eyes.

"And you think," she asked softly, "your gift of this weekend, being an intangible gift, has no value?"

"Honey, I didn't—" Wolf began.

"You're right." His eyes widened slightly at the firm words that cut across his protest. Blinking against the hot moisture that clouded her eyes, Micki placed the tip of her finger over his mouth, silencing whatever he was about to say. "There can be no price tag attached to the gift you've given me, simply because, to me, this weekend has been priceless." Despite her efforts, two tears escaped, rolled slowly down her face. "I never dreamed this kind of happiness, this perfect contentment, was possible to achieve."

71

Her voice faltered and she lowered her eyes. Hesitant but determined, she went on softly. "This is the gift you've given me, Wolf, and that's why I was crying."

A stunned silence followed her small speech and Micki began to tremble, certain she'd shattered the harmony they'd shared till now.

"Good God, can this woman be real?" Wolf's hushed tone held a hint of genuine awe. Glancing up at him, Micki saw he was no longer looking at her, but was staring at the night-blackened porthole. As if unaware of her, he went on, in the same hushed tone. "She offers me her innocence, her youth, her trust, then absolves me with her tears for my greedy use of them."

In the shadowy light Micki thought she saw his eyelashes flutter suspiciously, then all thought stopped as she was hauled, almost roughly, into his arms.

"You can have no idea what your words mean to me," Wolf whispered raggedly, "because I have no idea where to begin to express my feelings. But what I said was true. I am greedy and I don't want to waste one minute of our time together."

They left the boat in a once-again mist-shrouded pre-dawn. Like the morning before, Micki woke to find Wolf getting dressed.

"Wolf?" The one softly murmured word held both a question and a plea for him to come back to bed.

"I was just going to wake you." Wolf's eyes devoured her. "It's time to go, baby."

"But, I don't—" Micki's protest died as his features settled into lines of hard determination. Trying a different tactic, she asked innocently, "Aren't you going to kiss me good morning?"

Although a smile curved his lips, he shook his head emphatically. "No way, honey. If I come over there, it'll be noon before we get off this tub. I want to get you home while there's at least a chance no one will see you, for if anyone even suspects we've spent the weekend together, your reputation will be shot to hell.''

"I don't care about that—" Micki began earnestly.

"I care." Wolf's tone was suddenly harsh. "And you should too." The fingers of his right hand raked through his hair and rubbed absently at the back of his neck. Wolf sighed and went on less harshly. "God, honey, I'm eleven years older than you. Can you imagine your father's reaction if he found out about this?"

Micki could, only too well. The thought alone sent a shudder rippling through her slender frame. She groaned softly.

"Exactly," Wolf said flatly. "At any other time I wouldn't give one goddamn what your father, or anyone else for that matter, thought about me. But right now I can't afford that unconcern. So don't argue, babe. I'm going to go make some coffee. By the time it's ready I want to see you in the galley fully"—his eyes shifted to her discarded bikini and beach coat and his tone went dry— "dressed."

They stepped off the boat into a pearl-white cloud. Halfway along the narrow pier Micki paused to look back at the apparitionlike outline of the craft, bobbing gently in the ruffling bay waters. When she turned back to Wolf, her face was wistful, her eyes sad. One strong arm encircled her waist, drew her close. Bending over her, he murmured, "We'll come back, honey."

Micki's eyes lit up. "When? Can we come back tonight?" The light dimmed as he slowly shook his head. Meekly, she walked beside him to the car park.

"Although I'm crazy about the way you look in a bikini, I want you to get all dressed up to go out for dinner tonight."

"Can't we have dinner on the boat?" The light was back and for a moment he didn't answer, seemingly bemused by the sparkling blue of her eyes.

"You'd rather have dinner on the boat than go out somewhere?" Wolf laughed.

"Yes," Micki answered gently. "Can we? Please?"

"You're absolutely something else, youngster." Wolf's tone shivered over her skin like a caress. He stopped walking and turned to her, his arm tautening as he crushed her to him. In complete opposition to his crushing hold, his kiss was a tender blessing that robbed her lungs of air, her legs of strength.

"All right, we'll have dinner on the boat." He started moving again, his arm possessive around her waist. "But I still want you to get dressed up. I'll come for you about eight. I have an appointment in Cape May this afternoon." He stopped beside a late-model Ford, unlocked the door, and held it open for her. Seated in the car, Micki watched him, loving the long, lean look of him, as he strode around the front of the car and slid into the seat beside her. Frowning, he turned to her. "If I can shorten the meeting, which I doubt, I'll call you. But I can't make any promises."

His tone held such finality Micki didn't have the courage to argue.

"All right, Wolf, you're the boss."

Her tone of meek acceptance amused him and a devilish grin flashed, revealing strong white teeth. "And don't you forget it," he drawled softly.

When he pulled up in front of her home, Wolf reached across her body to open her door, gave her a quick, hard kiss, and growled, "Get out of here, babe. I've got to get home and grab some rest or I'll be useless at the meeting this afternoon." The soulful eyes Micki lifted to his turned the growl into a groan. "Oh, God, baby, will you get out of the car?" His hands came up to cradle her face, his mouth was a hungrily searing brand. Then he moved back behind the wheel with an ordered, "Go."

Micki went, on the run, not stopping until she was inside her own bedroom. After stripping off the very wilted beachwear, she dove, stark naked, between the sheets. Laughing and crying at the same time, she hugged herself fiercely. Oh, Lord, she was so crazily, wildly in love with that man, it was almost scary.

She woke late in the afternoon, automatically reaching for the solid bulk of Wolf's body. When her hand found nothing but emptiness, she opened her eyes and sighed on finding herself in her own bed. Stifling a yawn, she stretched contentedly. The sensuous movement of her body between the smooth sheets evoked the sensuous thoughts of Wolf's expertly arousing hands and she gasped softly at the sudden, sharp ache that invaded the lower part of her body, the small hard points that thrust against the sheet covering her breasts. God, she was well and truly caught, she thought fearfully, if the mere thought of him could have this kind of effect.

Rolling her head on the pillow, she stared at the fake-gem-encrusted tiny alarm clock on her small nightstand. Two fifty-eight. Micki groaned aloud. Five hours until she'd see him. Kicking off the sheet, she jumped out of bed. She had to do something to fill those hours. Pulling on a light cotton duster, she left the room and went to the kitchen.

Forty-five minutes later, Micki stood at the sink, a small smile curving her lips, washing the dishes. She hadn't realized she was so hungry! It had required a large glass of orange juice, two poached eggs, three slices of toast, and three cups of coffee to appease her suddenly ravenous appetite.

Leaving the kitchen spotless, she went back to her room, made her bed, then headed for the bathroom for a shampoo and a shower. Humming softly as she stood under the warm shower spray, Micki didn't hear her father and Regina enter the house. She was standing before the medicine cabinet mirror, blow drying her hair, when her father tapped on the door and called, "Hi, honey, will you be very long? I feel the need of a shower."

Shutting the dryer off, Micki disconnected the plug and opened the door. "Hi, Dad," she said as she leaned toward him and kissed his whisker-rough cheek. "Welcome home, have a good trip?"

"Gruesome," Bruce grimaced. "You know what New York is like in August. Why the hell these realtors had to have their conference there is beyond me." He sighed wearily. "I was tied up in meetings most of the time, which didn't do a thing for Regina's patience. She should have listened to me and stayed at home."

Fleetingly, and for the first time since her father's marriage, Micki thanked the powers-that-be for Regina's stubbornness. "Well, you're home now and the bathroom's all yours. You can have your shower. And, Dad"—one slim hand caressed his cheek—"have a shave too."

"Brat." A larger hand made contact with her bottom.

Smiling happily, Micki went to her room. She was plugging the blow dryer into the wall socket by her dressing table when the phone rang. Wolf! The dryer dropped onto the table's mirror-bright surface with a clatter as Micki ran across the room. Flinging the door wide, she dashed along the hall and started down the stairs.

"Hello."

Micki was halfway down the stairs when she heard Regina answer the phone. She took one more step down then froze, her hand gripping the railing at Regina's velvety, incredibly sexy-sounding words.

"Wolf, darling, couldn't you wait? We haven't been in the house a half hour. I know how impatient you are and I was about to call you."

Eyes widening in disbelief, Micki waited breathlessly through the small silence while Regina listened to whatever Wolf was saying. When she spoke again, her words sent a shaft of pure hatred through Micki.

"The trip was exactly as you warned me it would be— dreadful. I could have kicked myself for not staying here to go with you as you wanted me to." There was another

76

short pause, then, "Bruce? No, he's having a shower, how could he know? I told you we just got in. Yes, of course, darling, I want that as badly as you do."

Feeling she couldn't bear to hear any more, Micki, moving like a zombie, started back up the stairs. The sound of her name stopped her.

"Micki? No, she's not here. But then, she rarely ever is." Regina paused to listen again, then replied with a sigh, "I don't know, possibly with Tony Menella, she's been seeing a lot of him lately. She does not confide in me, but I'm sure she doesn't know."

Ordering her numbed body to move, Micki retraced her steps to her bedroom. Standing in the middle of the room, she stared sightlessly at the wall. Wolf and Regina? The words became a tortured scream in her mind.

Wolf and Regina? Oh, dear God, could Regina be one of the women who had cried on receiving a gift, usually expensive, from Wolf? Shaking all over, Micki blinked her eyes and when she did, her gaze touched the bed. Hot color flared into her cheeks on the thought that Wolf had robbed her father like an outlaw. First his wife, now his daughter.

Choking back the bitter gall that rose in her throat, Micki silently berated herself. *You fool, you young, stupid, virginal fool. Correction,* she thought, fighting against a growing hysteria, *ex-virginal fool.*

"Micki?"

The sound of Regina's soft voice, followed by a gentle tap on her door, turned the budding hysteria into cold fury. Before she could answer, the door was opened and Regina entered the room, closing the door behind her.

"I thought you were out. Have you been in your room all this—"

"What do you want?" The voice that slashed across Regina's words held cold contempt and a new maturity.

"Micki." Regina hesitated, then asked bluntly, "Were

77

you out with Wolf Renninger while your father and I were away?"

"That's none of your business." Striding across the room, Micki brushed by Regina on her way to the door. At the contact, her duster parted at her throat, revealing the abrasions David's plundering mouth had left on her skin.

"Did Wolf do that?" Regina gasped, pointing at the dull red mark.

"That's also none of your business," Micki snapped, one hand covering the spot. "I want you to leave my room." Her other hand grasped the doorknob to yank the door open but released it again at Regina's sharp words.

"You are a fool."

Spinning to face her, Micki looked her straight in the eye and spat, "Aren't we all?"

"Micki, you don't know this man." Regina's tone held an oddly pleading note. "Believe me, he lives up to his name. The women buzz around him like fleas at a honey pot. I must make this my business if you're to be kept from being hurt."

"I can take care of myself." Micki actually had to fight the urge to laugh in Regina's face. Hurt? Regina didn't know the meaning of the word.

"With a man like Wolf?" Regina asked, then answered her own question. "I hardly think so. He told me he was picking you up at eight." At Micki's nod a strange, almost crafty look entered her eyes. Very softly she said, "Don't be surprised if he's—well—somewhat tired. Or were you aware of the fact that he's spent the afternoon with a woman in Cape May? He was calling from her home actually."

Micki didn't want to believe her, but how could Regina know he was in Cape May unless he'd told her? Sickness churning in her stomach, Micki fought to maintain a cool facade. Wanting to get Regina out of the room before she

78

humiliated herself by throwing up in front of her, Micki waved her hand airily, forced herself to laugh lightly.

"I had no intention of going out with him," she lied. "I told him I would to get rid of him." Drawing a deep breath, she rushed on. "Do me a favor, Regina. When Wolf comes, tell him I'm out," she paused, then added, "with Tony."

CHAPTER 5

A chill rippled through Micki's body, partly from the dampness, partly from her thoughts. Tugging the edges of the sweater together, she stood up and went into the house. After locking the doors and hanging the sweater in the closet, she went up the stairs slowly, her face blank of expression, her eyes dull.

Six years! For six long years she'd suppressed all thoughts of him. And now, after being home only one day, he filled her mind to the exclusion of everything else. Why? Why had he been on the street at the exact time she stopped for that car? If she hadn't seen him, spoken to him. But she had seen him, had spoken to him. More stupid still, she had snapped at his tauntingly tossed bait.

Closing her bedroom door quietly, she walked across the darkened room, sank wearily into the fanned-back peacock chair, clasped her hands tightly in her lap. She was trembling all over and she felt sick to her stomach, as sick as she'd felt that night.

She had not gone with him that night, had not seen him. But she had heard him. From her bedroom doorway, she'd heard her father, innocently, for he really thought what he said was the truth. *Tell Wolf that she'd gone out with Tony Menella.* And she'd heard Wolf reply, "But we had a date for dinner," his voice rough with anger and confusion.

A shudder shook Micki's slender body. Closing her eyes, she rested her head back against the smooth wicker. He had called every day during that following week, and each time either Regina or her father told him the same thing. She was with Tony. She hadn't been, of course. She'd been hiding in her bedroom like a fugitive. And like a fugitive on the run, she stole away the next week without seeing him or talking to him again. Her father never knew the real reason she insisted on going back to school early.

But running away had not ended it. Oh, he had not tried to see her at school or contact her in any way, but he was with her in more ways than one. Although remembering the hurt caused actual pain, she had been unable to stop thinking about him. The feel of him, the scent of him, the taste of him, was in her blood and no amount of self-determination had succeeded in repelling him. And then, four weeks after she'd returned to school, she knew the life of him was inside her too.

Strangely, the realization that his child was growing inside her body banished the pain, replaced the hurt with deep contentment. She'd decided that even if she could not have the man, she could, and would, cherish his seed. There would be problems, not the least of which was her father, but thoughts of the baby had eased the ache in her heart and she grew daily more determined to have it.

Her euphoria had lasted two weeks. A euphoria only slightly dampened by her sudden aversion to eggs in the morning. Then horrible cramping pain in the middle of one night and a sticky, wet, red-stained sheet had burst her bubble of happiness. When she wakened in a hospital near the campus, one look at the faces of the doctor and nurse who were beside her bed told the story. She was one again, her body had repelled Wolf's issue. It was while she lay

82

in that sterile room alone, once again hurting unbearably, that her mind repelled Wolf's image.

No one except the hospital personnel knew of the abortion and three weeks after her twentieth birthday she left school. Luckily she had found a job and a room within a week of her arrival in Wilmington. She had not gone back until her father's illness two years ago. At that time she had not seen Wolf, nor had his name been mentioned. She had assumed he was no longer there, had moved on to greener pastures.

Over the years she had dated at least a dozen different men. And, in fact, was seeing one man exclusively before she came home. His name was Darrel and he'd asked her to marry him. She had been completely honest with him, without mentioning a name or circumstances. He knew he would not be the first, yet he'd asked her to marry him. Darrel was handsome, and Darrel was rich, and Darrel was successful. The perfect answer to any young woman's romantic dreams. But Micki was not any young woman. She had left him in Wilmington, two nights before, with her promise to think about his proposal.

Micki moved her head restlessly back and forth against the wicker, not even attempting to wipe away the tears that ran freely down her face. She knew what her answer to Darrel would be. She liked him, she respected him, but she did not love him. She loved Wolf. It was crazy. It was stupid. It was also an irrevocable fact. Nothing that had happened over the last six years had changed that. Within two nights and one day he had wrapped himself immovably around her heart. She had suspected even then that she would always love him. Now there was no doubt in her mind at all, and she could not go to Darrel loving Wolf.

Sighing softly, Micki stood up and began to undress. She would have to contact Darrel soon, give him her answer, and that answer would have to be no.

In sudden anger Micki tossed her clothes into the ham-

83

per, tugged a silky nightie over her head, and flung herself across her bed. Burying her face in her pillow, she wept quietly, damning the night she'd laid eyes on Wolf Renninger, damning the love for him that consumed her, and damning her own stupidity in accepting his challenge. She had been all right as long as she could not see him, be near him. But she knew that if she went with him Friday night it would just be a matter of time before she found herself in his arms, and in his bed, again. The urge to surrender that had swept through her that fateful afternoon had been all the proof she needed. She loved him and in loving him she wanted him desperately.

Rolling onto her back, Micki brushed impatiently at the tears on her cheeks. For six years she had repressed all her normal physical wants and needs. She had been called frigid. Some had even suggested therapy was called for. Micki had laughed at some and ignored them all. She knew exactly how normal her response could be. She had felt the hunger fire her blood. That hunger was for one man only. She had found the kisses, the light caresses, of several men pleasing. But only one man's mouth and hands could set her whole being alight. And now that one man, that Wolf, was stalking her again.

"No!"

The firm exclamation sounded loud in the dark room. Sitting up in the middle of the bed, Micki clenched her hands into fists. She could not go through that pain again. She would not expose herself to it. This time when Wolf came to pick her up she really would not be home. The decision made, Micki lay down again and went to sleep.

On Thursday Micki called the shop in Atlantic City to ask if it would be convenient for her to stop in sometime Friday afternoon. The enthusiastic reception her request was met with left her with a feeling of deep satisfaction.

Friday afternoon she bathed and dressed with extra care, then went looking for Regina to tell her she would not be home for dinner.

"If Cindy or anyone calls," she tossed casually over her shoulder, as she headed for the door, "tell them I expect to be late getting home and I'll return their call tomorrow."

Not wanting to field any questions Regina might throw, she hurried out the door and into her car. During the drive up the coast she determinedly pushed all thoughts of Wolf and his possible reaction to her action out of her mind.

It was a beautiful, hot day, the sun a bold yellow disc in a cloudless, blatantly blue sky. A day, Micki thought reminiscently, for healthy young things to laugh and romp on the scorching hot sand.

After parking the car near the hotel in which the shop was located, Micki walked along slowly, craning her neck like a tourist at the many changes that had taken place in the years since she'd last been in the city. So many of the old familiar buildings along the long boardwalk were gone, replaced by the large, elaborate hotels. The air literally reverberated with the sounds of construction.

Inside the hotel the air hummed a different tune. The place was crowded with people, all, it seemed, with one objective in mind—to get into the casino as quickly as possible.

Weaving in and out of the throng, Micki made her way to the reception desk. The cool, unruffled young man behind the desk gave her directions to the boutique politely, while running a practiced eye over her face and figure. When she thanked him, equally politely, he gave her an engaging grin and asked if she was free that evening.

"No, sorry," Micki grinned back. "I have an appointment."

"Why is it always some other guy that has all the luck?" He smiled sadly, then turned to the very impatient lady standing next to Micki.

The short exchange amused her, and with a jaunty step Micki walked through the lobby to the escalator the young man had indicated. As the steps moved up, her eyes roamed over the interior of the casino. The room was huge yet, incredibly, every square inch appeared to be occupied by humanity.

At the top of the escalator Micki paused to get her bearings. Directly across from her was the small cocktail lounge the desk clerk had mentioned, so the boutique should be a little farther down this wide expanse of hall. She found the shop exactly where he'd said she would.

With a knowledgeable eye Micki studied the displays inside the small windows on either side of the entrance to the shop. The one window proclaimed sun and fun with slightly reduced summer togs. The other window was a forecast of coming fall with soft plaid skirts and cashmere blazers. Very nice, Micki mused, very, very nice.

The manager of the shop turned out to be the woman Micki had spoken to the day before, and she was turned out very well indeed. A few years older than Micki, the woman, though not really beautiful, gave a good impression of being so. Her hair was a natural flaming red. Her skin a sun-kissed ivory. She was taller than Micki and her very slender body was beautifully clothed in an exquisite raw silk sheath that had Micki murmuring a silent prayer of thanks for the urge that had made her dress with such care.

While Micki had been studying the woman, the redhead had been making her own evaluation and they seemed to reach the same conclusions at exactly the same time. For just as Micki was giving thanks, the redhead smiled and extended a slim, long-nailed hand.

"Jennell Clark," she offered in a soft drawl. "And you must be Micki Durrant."

"I am." The hand Micki stretched out was just as slim, the rounded nails every bit as long. "How do you do?"

"Very well, actually." Jennell's soft laugh was a delight to the ears. "Glad to have you with us." Her eyes ran over Micki again. "If you buy for the shop as well as you buy for yourself I have a feeling I'll be doing even better."

"Thank you," Micki laughed with her. "I'll do my best." Then unable to exactly place the soft drawl in Jennell's tone, she asked, "Are you from the South?"

"Yes," Jennell again favored her with a laugh. "But not too far south, Richmond, Virginia. Where are you from?"

"Only a little south of here," Micki grinned. "Ocean City, New Jersey."

Jennell introduced her to the shop's other two employees, a petite, pretty young woman named Lucy and a strikingly beautiful black woman named Georgine. The three of them filled Micki in on the running of the store in no time.

The rest of the afternoon flew by so quickly, Micki was surprised when Jennell said it was time to close the shop. She was on the point of saying good-bye when Jennell asked, "Do you have plans for dinner? I mean do you have a date or are you expected home or anything?"

Micki thought fleetingly of Wolf, then shook her head. "No, no date or plans or anyone expecting me."

"Then come have dinner with us," Jennell coaxed. "Lucy's guy is out of town. Georgine's between guys and I"—an impish smile curved her red lips—"I'm punishing my man at the moment."

"Punishing?" Micki laughed.

"Well, just a little," the redhead drawled. "He was getting much too possessive and I'm letting him know I won't be owned. Will you come?"

As both Lucy and Georgine added their pleas to Jennell's, Micki agreed and the four of them left the shop, all talking at the same time.

They had dinner in a small restaurant where the decor was unexceptional and the food out of this world. While they ate, Micki learned that all three women came from other shops in the chain. Jennell from one in Washington, D.C., Lucy from one in Baltimore, and Georgine from one in New York City.

"I've been here for over a year," Jennell volunteered.

87

"Georgine came a few months after I did and Lucy joined us three months ago. Your predecessor came from Philadelphia at the same time as I did." She fluttered her lashes dramatically, drawled oversweetly. "She's been transferred to Miami." Jennell smiled derisively. "She went too far with the boss."

"You didn't like her?" Micki's question was greeted by rolled eyes and snorts of laughter.

"Honey," Jennell drawled softly, "I could sooner like a rattlesnake."

"She really wasn't very pleasant to work with." This from the small, somewhat shy, Lucy.

"She was a first-rate bitch," Georgine, every inch as worldly as she was beautiful, stated flatly.

"Yes," Jennell concurred. "Our buyer decided to play footsie with the owner. He shipped her out when she became demanding. I mean"—the drawl was laid on thick —"one just does not fool around with that man. Let alone demand marriage."

Micki frowned. When Jennell had said the boss, Micki assumed she'd been referring to their regional manager, Hank Carlton. But she'd just now said the owner and Micki had never met the owner, had not, in fact, ever heard his name mentioned. She was about to ask Jennell who the owner was when Lucy said something about finding a new man for Georgine and the thought went out of her head.

Their suggestions to Georgine ran from the ridiculous from Lucy.

"You could take an ad in the personal column like: Wanted: good-looking man between the ages of twenty-five and forty, must be fantastic dancer." To Micki she confided, "Georgine would rather dance than eat."

To the outrageous from Jennell.

"You could always station yourself on the boardwalk and smile sweetly at all the better-looking men. Of course," she drawled heavily, "you'd have no idea which

88

ones could dance. But then, look at all the fun you could have teaching them."

"The way my luck's been running," Georgine grinned, "if I took a newspaper ad I'd only get replies from the uglies and the crazies." The grin grew wider and her eyes sparkled impishly. "And if I stationed myself on the boardwalk, I'd probably wind up with my fanny in the canny."

A smile teased Micki's lips as she drove home that evening. She had enjoyed the dinner and the company very much. They had lingered, laughing, over their coffee until the arched look of the proprietor sent them, still laughing, out of the restaurant.

The three women had insisted on escorting Micki to her car, where they stood talking for an additional twenty minutes. By the time Micki drove her car off the parking lot she felt as if she'd known them all her life.

She'd had a good time, she told herself as she drove the car up the driveway of her father's house, a very good time. She had hardly thought about Wolf all evening, she realized as her fingers turned the key, shutting off the engine. Well, she mentally qualified, she hadn't thought about him too often, she admitted as she pulled on the hand brake. So, okay, he'd been in her thoughts constantly, she finally confessed disgustedly as she swung out of the car and headed for the kitchen door. But she had enjoyed her day and her evening.

"That you, princess?" her father called as she closed the door.

"No," Micki called back. "I'm a burglar, I've come for the silver."

"Good luck," he laughed. "We are strictly a stainless-steel family."

"Well, in that case, I guess I'll go back to being the princess." Micki smiled, entering the living room. "At least I'll have a title, even if there is no silver to inherit."

"Hi, honey." Although her father smiled, one brow

went up in question. "Did you forget you had a date this evening?"

"A date?"

Even with the sudden acceleration of her pulse, Micki had somehow managed to keep her tone innocent.

"With Wolf Renninger," Bruce prompted gently, then he winced. "I wouldn't say he was exactly happy when I told him you weren't here." He paused, his eyes narrowing in thought. "I had the oddest feeling that I'd gone through the same thing before." A frown leveled his brows. "What are you up to, young lady?"

"I—I'm not up to anything," Micki murmured nervously. She hated deceiving her father, yet she couldn't bring herself to confide in him. "I got caught up in the business of the shop and when the shop manager asked me to join her and the two women who work in the store, I accepted. I simply forgot I'd made the date with Wolf."

Micki wet her dry lips, trying not to see the sharp-eyed glance Regina gave her. Her father's memory might be a little cloudy, but Regina's certainly wasn't.

"Wolf has called twice in the last hour," Regina supplied quietly. "He seemed to be becoming angrier every time I had to tell him you hadn't come home yet."

"I think if the phone rings you had better answer it," Bruce advised. "You forgot the date and you can apologize your way out of it."

The words were no sooner out of his mouth when the doorbell rang. Micki's body jerked as though someone had touched a live wire to her.

"Go to it, girl." Her father flipped his hand in the direction of the front door. "I think there's little doubt who that is." He stood up, his hand reaching for Regina's. "We'll be discreet and give you some privacy."

The bell sounded again and Micki started for the door, her steps betraying her trepidation. Her father's soft laugh sounded from the stairs.

"You're not going to the gallows, honey," he chided.

"Just give him your sweetest smile and he'll forget why he's angry."

I'll bet, Micki thought grimly, her hand shaking as she reached for the doorknob. She swung the door open bravely, then bit her lip fearfully. Wolf, looking hard-jawed and cold-eyed and madder than hell, stood, hands thrust into his pants pockets, staring balefully at her. Stepping out onto the porch, Micki closed the door softly behind her, her mind searching for something to say. Wolf brought her search to an end.

"I don't believe it." His cool tone, so opposed to the hot anger in his eyes, sent a tremor bouncing down her spine. "I really don't believe it."

"What?" Micki was almost afraid to ask.

"You did it again." A touch of wonder colored the cool tone. "Do you get your kinky little kicks out of standing up many of your dates, or do I alone hold that honor?"

"Wolf." Micki had to fight to keep her voice even. "I'm sorry."

"Yeah." Wolf smiled crookedly. "I'll bet you are."

"All right, I'm not," Micki snapped. "If you'll recall, I didn't want to go out with you in the first place."

Angry herself now, she moved away from him, down the porch steps, and along the front walk to the pavement without the slightest idea of where she was going.

"But you did agree to have dinner with me." His long strides brought him alongside her before she'd taken six steps on the pavement. "Didn't you?"

"Yes," she admitted, turning south when she reached the corner.

Matching his stride to hers, Wolf walked beside her silently. *At least he didn't ask me where I'm going,* she thought wryly.

"Where the hell are you going?"

His impatient words followed on the heels of her thought and Micki couldn't repress the smile that tugged at her lips.

"I said something funny?" His tone was not amused.

"No," Micki sighed. "It's just that I don't know where I'm going."

"That's pretty damned obvious," Wolf drawled sardonically, leaving little doubt in her mind he meant the direction of her life, not her impromptu walk.

"I just felt like walking," Micki shrugged in annoyance.

"I see," Wolf drawled softly.

"You didn't have to come along," she snapped irritably.

"True," he agreed, with a maddening calmness.

Their quick stride ate up the blocks during their exchange and when they had to stop at a corner to wait for traffic Micki realized with surprise that they were near the city's shopping district. Grasping her arm, Wolf began walking east.

"Where the hell are *you* going?" Micki flung his words back at him.

"To the boardwalk," he answered imperturbably.

"Whatever for?" she demanded.

"Why does anyone stroll the boards?" She shrugged, elegantly. "To gaze at the ocean, to feel the sea breeze against the skin, to wander in and out of the shops." He slanted a barbed look at her. "To have something to eat. At least those who have been stood up and didn't eat any dinner do."

His hand placed firmly at the back of her waist propelled her up the ramp and onto the boardwalk still crowded with people at ten o'clock at night.

"Come on, babe, I'll buy you a slice of pizza at Mack and Manco's." His eyes raked her face. "Not exactly what I'd planned but," he shrugged, "I like the pie and it will fill up the hole in my stomach."

Unsure if he was telling the truth or not about not having eaten, Micki allowed him to lead her to the pizza stand. The stand's outside counter was three deep with people and, grasping her hand, Wolf edged around the bodies and drew her inside the shop. While they waited for two seats to become vacant Micki watched, as fascinated as she'd been as a young girl, the swift, dexterous movements of the young men behind the counter as they assembled the pizzas and slid them into and out of the ovens. And the aroma! Even though she'd had dinner, Micki ran her tongue over her lips in anticipation.

Once seated, they were served quickly and Micki was soon convinced Wolf had not been lying about not eating. He consumed four slices of pizza to her one and as soon as they were out of the shop said, "Let's walk awhile, then we'll hunt up some dessert."

"On top of all that pizza!" Micki exclaimed.

"Look at me, Micki," Wolf urged chidingly. "Tom Thumb I'm not. I've got a big body and it's got to be filled occasionally. It is now"—he glanced at his watch—"ten thirty-five. That pizza was the first solid food I've had since somewhere around noon." His tone went bland. "Yes, I am going to sink some dessert on top of all that pizza."

"Solid food?" Micki jabbed at him, as if that's all she'd heard of his statement.

"Did I ask you if you'd been drinking?" Wolf jabbed back harder.

Fuming, Micki walked beside him, uncomfortably aware he was laughing, if silently, at her. After several quiet minutes, curiosity and a concern she didn't want to feel got the better of her.

"Were you drinking, Wolf," she asked softly, "on an empty stomach?"

"I had a couple of beers in a bar over at the Point," Wolf replied equally softly. "To pass the time while I waited for my date to put in an appearance."

Feeling her face flush, Micki looked away from him and glanced into the faces of the people moving around them. Up until that point her mind had been so full of Wolf she'd been only surfacely aware of the hum of voices, the sound of laughter around her. Tugging her hand free of his grasp, she walked to the rail and stared out at the dark, white-capped water.

"Why didn't you keep our date?"

Wolf bent his long frame beside her, rested his forearms on the top rail, propped one foot on the bottom rail. He had removed his suit jacket and it dangled in the air over the beach, held in the fingers of one hand.

Micki's eyes clung to the gentle movement of the jacket, held so carelessly in those strong fingers. Not unlike the way he handles women, Micki thought suddenly, a shiver feathering her back. The idea of being held in those strong hands, even carelessly, made her feel sick with longing.

"I asked you a question." Wolf's edged tone jolted her back to reality.

"I went up to Atlantic City this afternoon to introduce myself to the manager of the shop I've been transferred to," Micki explained nervously. "We got talking shop talk and the time slipped away. By the time the shop closed, I'd forgotten about our date and when she asked me if I'd like to have dinner with her and the other two women who work there, I said yes."

"You are a very bad liar, babe," Wolf grated, not looking at her. "Now would you like to tell me the real reason?"

"Honestly, Wolf, you are—" Micki began angrily.

"Honestly?" He cut her off. "I don't think so, sweetie. I honestly think you've been lying through your teeth. Why the hell won't you level with me? Did you go out with another guy?" He was on the attack now and Micki felt cornered by his stinging tone. "Someone you ran into after you agreed to go with me? If so, why the hell didn't you call me and break the date?"

Micki turned to face him, her eyes bright with anger. "Would you have let me break the date?"

Wolf's silvery eyes turned the color of cold steel as he stared into hers. "Probably not," he finally snapped, after a few long, nerve-racking seconds.

"That's what I thought." Micki wrenched her eyes from his, stared sightlessly out over the ocean. "So I simply decided not to keep it."

"*Were* you with another man?" Wolf's tone held a strange, breathless quality Micki couldn't define. For a brief moment she considered telling him she had been out with another man, then she sighed and murmured, "No."

She heard her sigh echo beside her before his voice, close to her ear, sent tiny little chills skimming over her body.

"What are you afraid of, honey?"

"Wh-what do you mean?" she stammered. "Afraid of?"

"Are you afraid, if you go with me, I'll get you alone and want to touch you?" His breath fluttered the hair near her ear; his words started a fluttering in her mid-section. "Afraid I'll want to hold you in my arms and kiss you?" His voice went low. "Afraid I'll want to make love to you?"

Micki's hands gripped the rail. She couldn't answer, she couldn't move. In fact, she could hardly breathe.

"You'd be right." Wolf's voice was very low now, low and urgent. "I do want to do all those things."

Motionless, unseeing, Micki stood as if fused to the boards beneath her feet, the need to have him do all those things draining all the color from her face. Oh, God, how she ached to be in his arms, and yes, in his bed. Her own thoughts frightened her into action. Pushing herself away from the rail, she dashed across the boardwalk, dodging in and out, around the startled faces of people. Wolf caught up to her as she came off the ramp.

"Running away again?" His tone was now sharp with exasperation.

"I simply want to go home." Micki shrugged his hand from her arm. He slid it around her waist, held on tightly.

"What are you running from, do you know?" Wolf asked tiredly. "Did you know six years ago?"

"Shut up," Micki cried, then lowered her voice at the

95

sharp glance a man passing them threw at her. "I don't want to talk about six years ago. I don't even want to think about it."

"Why?" Wolf rapped softly. "Why don't you want to talk about it?" Micki was almost running in her urgent need to get home. Wolf tightened his hand at her waist even more, forcing her to slow down. "Why don't you want to think about it?"

"I told you why in your apartment the other day." Micki lied frantically. "It's dead and there's nothing as dead as a dead love affair."

Wolf came to an abrupt halt and grasped her shoulder to turn her toward him.

"So that's what it was," he rasped, "a love affair." His soft laughter had the sound of rusty metal being scraped. Micki felt fear clog her throat. "I'll give you a hundred dollars against a Mexican peso I can breathe life into it again." His fingers dug into her soft flesh to draw her closer. "What kind of gambler are you?"

His mouth touched hers and at that moment a car full of teenage boys drove by. Laughing and hooting, the boys called encouraging suggestions to Wolf and though he released her, he threw them a wicked grin.

Micki used his momentary inattention to move away from him. Wolf was right behind her.

"For God's sake, kid, slow down." His big hand swallowed hers, held fast. "I wasn't going to hurt you."

The mere thought of you hurts me, Micki's mind cried silently. Shaking her head to dislodge the thought, she said bitingly, "I know that, but I hate being put into a position to receive that kind of taunting catcall." She tried to tug her hand free, shot him a sour look when his fingers tightened. "And I'm not a kid."

"Then stop acting like one," he bit back. "Those boys didn't mean any harm." Micki withdrew into a stony silence. Walking steadily, her eyes straight ahead, she sighed with relief when they turned the corner onto her

96

street. She couldn't wait to get into the house for the simple reason she wanted to be with him so badly.

Wolf stopped, pulling her up short, several yards from the house. With a casual wave of his hand he indicated a flame-red Ferrari parked at the curb.

"Come have a drink with me," he coaxed. "I haven't had my dessert yet."

"I don't want a drink," Micki said flatly, swinging away from him again. "I'm not thirsty, I'm tired."

Hurrying up the front walk, she prayed her father had not come back downstairs and locked the door. She had to get away from Wolf. She knew it. She had been tempted to go with him, had wanted to go with him. And she knew that given even the few minutes it would take her father to come down and open the door for her, Wolf would be able to persuade her into going with him.

"Why are you so tired?" Wolf's hand on her arm made her pause in front of the door. "It's only eleven fifteen."

"I'm not physically tired, Wolf." Micki had not turned her head, and her words seemed to bounce off the door, back into her face.

Wolf's hand left her arm to circle her waist and she felt her throat go dry when he stepped closer to her. With trembling fingers she clutched the doorknob as if grasping for a lifeline.

"Micki, baby." Wolf's soft voice, only inches from her ear, was a nerve-shattering temptation. "If you're not really tired, come with me."

"But I am really tired," Micki insisted in a dry, crackling voice. Her hand turned the knob and pushed, relief washing over her when the door gave under pressure. "I'm tired of this conversation. I'm tired of defending myself." Turning her head, she forced herself to meet his gaze levelly. "I'm tired of your company, Wolf."

Wolf stepped back as if she'd actually struck him. His face drained of all expression and quite a bit of color. His lips thinned. His eyes narrowed.

"Okay, baby." His lips barely seemed to move around the muttered words. "I guess you can't make it any clearer than that." He turned away, started down the porch steps, then turned back swiftly. "But if you change your mind, you'll have to call me. I won't be calling you." His lips twisted, almost as if he were in pain. His voice rasped against her ears. "I've had about all I can take of your brand of rejection."

Micki gasped audibly. Stung by what she considered was the unfairness of his taunting words, she retaliated without thinking.

"Don't hold your breath."

"Very classy," Wolf drawled stingingly. "And you say you're not a kid. You've said very little to prove otherwise tonight."

His silvery eyes, sharp with scorn, moved dismissively over her body, then, with a shrug, he turned away again. Hurt unbearably by his sarcastic words and the scorn in his eyes, Micki was goaded into trying to hurt back.

"If you hurry, Wolf," she called softly, as he started down the walk, "you can drink a gallon of dessert before the bar closes."

"Grow up, kid," Wolf tossed back disparagingly, not even bothering to look back.

CHAPTER 6

Wolf's parting shot nagged at Micki's mind for most of the following week. She just could not decide what exactly he'd meant by it. Not "Grow up, kid." She understood that well enough. But the prior one, the one about his having had enough of her brand of rejection, that bothered her. She was sure the gibe could not be taken at face value, for that would indicate his being hurt, and that concept she could not accept.

During that week, the last of her vacation, Micki kept very busy and away from Regina's questioning eyes. She spent hours on the beach, soaking up sun, acquiring a deep tan that made her eyes look an even brighter blue. She saw, or spoke on the phone to every one of her friends still at home, including Tony, who called and asked her to have dinner with him on Saturday night. She accepted eagerly for two reasons. One, she would be truly delighted to see Tony again and two, she was ready to jump at any excuse to get out of the house.

Determined to keep her mind occupied every waking minute, she lived that week on the run. From house to beach, back to the house to shower, then out again to have lunch or shop with Cindy, or visit her old haunts. For several hours on Tuesday afternoon she lost herself in the nineteenth century by way of the Historical Museum. All other thoughts were sent packing as her imagination was caught, then consumed, by the lifelike reality of the priceless antique furniture and household articles used in the display areas set up as living room, dining room, bedroom, kitchen, and nursery.

A small smile tugged at her bemused expression as she imagined herself and her friends dressed in the apparel worn at the turn of the century, carefully preserved and kept in glass cases, in the Fashion Room.

As she moved slowly through the Sindia Room, she could almost feel the anxiety of the crew of the four-masted bark when it was driven onto the beach in a gale on December 15, 1901.

The contemplative state induced by her visit into yesteryear stayed with her through the remainder of the day and evening and left her with the surety that an individual life was indeed too short to be wasted.

On Thursday evening she agreed to go with her father and Regina to the Music Pier for the concert given nightly by the Ocean City Pops. Her father and Regina went inside the large building on the pier while Micki sat on a bench outside as she had years before, watching the ocean's constant movement while she listened to the music.

The strains of Rodgers and Hammerstein music, blending with the muted roar of the sea, evoked memories of her girlhood. In the years she'd been away, she hadn't consciously realized how much she'd missed it all. And now, the atmosphere, the ambience, seemed to seep through her skin into her heart. Irrevocably her wandering thoughts led to Wolf.

Moving restlessly on the slatted wood bench, she fought in vain against the image that would no longer be pushed away. Silvery eyes mocked her struggle. Sighing softly, Micki closed her eyes while the essence of him took control of her senses, her emotions. Where was he tonight? What was he doing? Most importantly, who was he doing it with? Her own thoughts bedeviled and hurt her, yet she could no longer keep them at bay. She was resentful, hurt, jealous of his activities, his companions, even though she knew she had no right to be. She loved him distractedly, passionately, and that love had the effect of slashing her to ribbons inside.

She needed him in every way, and the growing intensity of that need sparked near panic. With a sickening feeling of humiliation clogging her throat, Micki faced the realization that unless she found a way to dislodge his occupation of her mind she would be reduced to calling him, as he had suggested she should.

With determination spawned by desperation, she made plans for the rest of the summer, pushing aside the nagging reminder that the best laid plans . . . She had to overcome her emotional obsession with him. She had to—somehow. For one tiny moment she allowed herself the remembered breathlessness aroused by his arms, his mouth, then, with a quick, sad shake of her head she wished him to Siberia, or some other, much hotter, place.

The sound of the sea and the music lulling her into a somewhat dreamlike state of wishful thinking, Micki convinced herself of her eventual success. She would throw herself vigorously into her new job and fill her non-working hours by finding and settling into a new apartment. Even though she had made arrangements to have her things packed and trucked to her father's house when her lease ran out at the end of August, she could take a run up to Wilmington to oversee the removal. Born of desperation, ideas popped into her mind. There were any number of things she could do to stay busy and, she vowed fervently, she would do them, all of them, to escape the hold Wolf had on her.

Riding the crest of optimism as bravely as a surfer skimming a wave, Micki walked home from the concert with a jaunty stride, humming snatches of the music she'd heard.

"I get the distinct impression you enjoyed the concert," her father teased.

"Very much," Micki affirmed, flashing him a smile. "I always have. The tenor soloist was pretty good, at least what I could hear out at the rail sounded good."

"I liked the aria the soprano sang," Regina inserted quietly. "Even though I can't remember the name of it and your father knows absolutely nothing about opera. Do you know it, Micki?"

Know it? Micki hadn't even heard it. Shaking her head, she frowned.

"No, I'm sorry, Regina, I'm afraid I don't know any more about opera than Dad does."

"It doesn't matter really," Regina smiled. "It's just been tantalizing the edge of my memory, if you know what I mean?"

Did she ever, Micki groaned silently. When it came to a subject tantalizing the memory, she was an expert. Veering sharply from the thought, she launched into another song, singing where she knew the words, humming where she didn't.

"Do you have plans for the weekend, honey?" Bruce's soft voice cut into her slightly off-key version of "A Cockeyed Optimist."

"Yes," Micki nodded. "I've been invited to Cindy and Benny's for dinner tomorrow and I have a date with Tony Saturday."

Micki didn't miss the sharp-eyed glance Regina shot her at the mention of Tony's name. In an effort to block any questions from her stepmother, she rushed on. "Why? Was there something you wanted me to do?"

"No, no," Bruce assured her. "We were invited to a cookout Saturday evening and you were included, if you were free."

"A cookout? Where?" Micki asked curiously.

102

"At Betty and Jim Grant's," Regina answered for her husband. "Betty wanted to meet you and thought this might be a good time and way."

"And I would like to finally meet her," Micki assured her. For Micki, Regina's friend Betty had been a warm voice on the phone. They had become friends while Micki was away. Although she had not intruded at the time of Bruce's illness, her voice had been a bracing encouragement at the other end of the line during those nerve-racking days. "Ask her if I may have a raincheck."

"Not necessary," Bruce put in smoothly. "I would like you to keep two weeks from Saturday open, honey. There's a celebration party being planned for that night and, as the Grants will be there, you will meet Betty then."

"A celebration party?" Micki's brows went up. "For what?"

"A big-time developer and several realtors, myself included, are on the verge of closing a very big deal. It's been in the works for some time, and we decided a celebration was in order. We'd like you with us for two reasons. First, simply to have you join us in celebrating the successful conclusion to some very long, hard negotiations. And secondly, because it will be the last evening we'll spend together for a while as"—he paused to glance at his wife—"Regina and I will be flying to the West Coast the following afternoon."

"You're actually going?" Micki cried happily. "Terrific. How long will you be gone? Where are you going? I mean, are you going to stay in Frisco the whole time or are you planning to take in other places—Vegas, Mexico?"

"I believe you are nearly as excited as we are," Bruce laughed when Micki finally ran down. They were almost home and as they turned onto the front walk he dropped an arm around her shoulders. "The minute we get into the house we'll show you our itinerary."

He removed his arm to unlock the door. "We plan to be gone the last two weeks of August." With a wide courtly sweep of his arm he ushered them inside. "So will you go to the party with us?"

"Yes, of course, if you want me to go," Micki answered quickly. "Now, lead me to your itinerary."

They sat around the kitchen table, tall, moisture-beaded glasses of iced tea in front of them, until after midnight, Regina and Bruce talking at the same time, cutting in on each other as they outlined their plans for Micki.

For Micki, Friday evening was an unqualified success. Cindy had gone all out in her preparations for dinner and the dining-room table gleamed with her best china and crystal (Micki's wedding gift to them). The menu complemented the entrée of fried chicken. The consommé was delicious, the small parslied potatoes cooked to just the right peak, and the tiny creamed peas and pearl onions tender. For dessert Cindy served a rich homemade cheesecake Micki was sure she could not possibly manage, but she did.

"Is this the same girl who could not boil an egg seven years ago?" Micki asked Benny with not altogether mock surprise.

"Can you believe it?" Benny laughed. "You should see the pile of cookbooks this woman has collected." His eyes caressed Cindy's face. "She has been a very busy lady since you left, Micki. She's learned to sew so well she now makes most of her own clothes and now she is knitting." His tone was so full of pride, his eyes so full of tenderness as he gazed at his wife, Micki felt the hot sting of tears behind her lids. "I swear," he murmured, "she began knitting tiny things the day after she conceived."

"You big oaf, will you stop?" Cindy's glowing face proclaimed her love as she chided Benny. "You're embarrassing me."

"Why?" Benny's hand caught and held Cindy's tightly. "Because I love you and I don't care who knows it?" He lifted her hand to his lips, bestowed a light kiss before adding, "Besides which, Micki's our friend, our best friend, why would you be embarrassed before her?"

"Oh, Benny."

Cindy's half sigh, half whisper brought a lump to Micki's throat and in an attempt to dislodge it she drawled dryly, "I can do a fantastic disappearing act if you two want to be alone."

"Would you?" Benny teased.

"Don't you dare," Cindy gasped.

The banter flew back and forth all evening. The closest they came to a serious subject was while they considered the best location for Micki to begin her apartment hunting.

Micki was in a mellow mood when she left and as she drove along the almost deserted streets a gentle smile curved her lips. Cindy and Benny were so perfectly suited and so obviously in love it was a joy just being in their company. Who would have believed it, back when Cindy was tossing insults at Benny every five minutes? Had, Micki wondered, Cindy been attracted to him even then? Very likely, Micki decided. The insults and taunts were probably the adolescent Cindy's way of venting that attraction. And Benny? Micki's smile grew tender remembering how good-naturedly he had taken Cindy's constant ribbing. What a delight they were to be with, Micki mused. If only Wolf were . . . Micki put a brake on her thoughts abruptly. Scathingly she told herself *if only* must surely be the most overworked words in the English language. You can *if only* from now until the first day of forever, she scolded herself mentally, and it will change nothing. So forget it. Forget him.

Her date with Tony the following evening was a mixture of fun and sadness. The fun began the minute she opened the door to him, for she was caught in his arms and twirled around in the air.

"Micki." Tony laughed down at her when she stood once more firmly on the floor. "You look as gorgeous as ever, only more so. God, what a sight you are for these weary old eyes."

"Weary old eyes, my Aunt Sara," Micki laughed back. "It's good to see you too, Tony. What are you up to these days?"

"Oh, about five-eleven," Tony drawled. "Maybe six feet."

"I'd have been disappointed if you hadn't said that."

Although Micki's tone was teasing, there was an underlying note of seriousness to it. It was silly, she knew, yet she would have been disappointed. His predictable rejoinder had reaffirmed their friendship, their closeness.

She had been around twelve the first time he'd quipped the reply to her. It had been summer then, too, and on that afternoon Micki had felt deserted and alone as all her girl friends were otherwise occupied. Without much hope of finding a companion, she had scuffed her way forlornly to the playground. She had found the fourteen-year-old Tony, looking every bit as dejected and forlorn, leaning against the playground fence. He had been watching, with lofty teenage amusement, the antics of a group of toddlers and had not seen Micki approach.

"None of the kids are around today," Micki had grumbled as she leaned against the fence beside him. "What are you up to, Tony?"

Maybe it was the sound of abject self-pity in her voice. Micki never knew, but when Tony turned to look at her, all signs of his own dejection had vanished. His expression was one of consideration and when he answered his tone was serious.

"Oh, about five-three, maybe four."

"Huh?"

She was wrapped up in her own misery, so his quip had gone completely over her head. She had gazed up at him blankly for several seconds before the dancing gleam in his sky-blue eyes and the betraying shake of his skinny shoulders turned the light on in her head. Her reaction was way out of proportion to the humor in his remark. The young, very naive Micki became convulsed with laughter.

"You goof!" she had gasped when her giggles had subsided somewhat. Balling her hand into a small, tight fist, she swung it at his arm. Tony caught her by the wrist before her fist made contact and shook it gently.

"Come on, you silly ass." Tony's grin had held amusement, and a dash of superiority. "Since we're both alone, we may as well be alone together."

They had kept each other company for the rest of the day and until nine thirty that night. After they had plumbed all the diversions offered by the playground, they moved onto the beach and from there to the bay to watch the fishing boats return. From the bay they went to Tony's home where Micki had promptly been invited to supper. After a quick phone call to her father obtaining permission for her to stay, Micki and Tony earned their supper by pulling weeds out of his mother's flower bed. And from the time they left the supper table until Tony's dad ran her home at nine thirty, they had engaged in a hotly contested game of Monopoly—which Tony won.

From that day until Micki left to go back to college six years ago, their greeting to each other had been the nonsensical, "What are you up to?" the only variance being the inches in Tony's reply.

Now, they stood, one twenty-five, the other twenty-seven, laughing into each other's face exactly as they had all those years ago.

"Tony, you are still a goof." Micki shook her head sharply, fighting the tears of affection that suddenly threatened. Sliding her arms around his waist, she gave him a quick, hard hug. "Do you think we'll ever grow up?"

"God, I hope not," Tony murmured fervently into her hair, returning her hug fiercely. When he released her, he glanced around curiously. "Where's your dad and Regina?"

"At a cookout." Micki's laughter, finally under control, threatened to break out again at the crafty expression that stole over Tony's face.

"We're all alone here?" he whispered slyly.

"Yes," Micki whispered back. "Why?"

"You want to stay here?" he leered exaggeratedly. "Fool around a little." His voice went very low. "We could play doctor."

"No!" Micki exploded into gales of laughter all over again. Grasping his arm, she urged him toward the front door. "Come on, you nut, you asked me out to dinner, so let's go dine. I hope you brought an enormous amount of money with you because I'm starving."

"How much do you consider enormous?" Tony eyed her warily.

"Oh, at least twenty-five or thirty dollars," Micki said airily.

Tony exhaled a long, exaggerated sigh of relief as he stepped out onto the front porch. "You lucked out," he replied jauntily. "I think I have around thirty-two."

"Are you serious?" Micki turned to look at him, all traces of merriment erased from her face.

"Of course not," he chided gently. "When were we ever serious?"

They drove to an Italian restaurant in Wildwood, where Micki declared the food almost as good as Tony's mother's. Tony did most of the talking while they ate, telling about his job in Trenton, why he had decided to make the move home, and all about his present job and apartment.

A soft light in her eyes, Micki watched him while he talked, noting the changes in his face. He was, she decided, one fine-looking young man. His swarthy skin tone and wavy dark hair were set off, given an appealing look by his light-blue eyes and perfect white teeth. A small pale scar, earned in a high school football game, which broke the line of his left eyebrow, added a rakish touch to his visage. Yes, indeed, a very fine-looking young man.

After dinner Tony took Micki to a bar that catered to the dance crowd. The minute the waitress had taken their order and turned away from their minuscule table, Tony stood up and tugged at her arm.

"Come on, Micki, let's show them how it's done."

Tony had always been a good dancer and Micki quickly discovered he'd improved with age. Lithe, agile, he moved around the floor, and her, in a sensuously serpentine way.

From that afternoon in the playground Micki had never felt awkward with Tony, and after only a momentary hesitation, she gave herself fully to the music and the beat.

"Yeah, do it, girl," Tony encouraged, undulating smoothly in front of her. "Crank it up."

By the time they left the bar some four hours later, Micki's head was slightly fuzzy from a combination of the loud music and the drinks she'd consumed. Her body was damp with perspiration and she felt as if her legs might fall off at any moment.

As they drove back to Ocean City, Micki leaned her head back against the seat with a contented sigh. The breeze rushing in through the car's windows cooled her overheated skin and Micki inhaled deeply, savoring the scent of the sea.

"Do you want to come to my place and see my etchings?" Tony's quiet voice nudged her out of a half doze.

"Do you have some?" Micki asked innocently with deliberately widened eyes.

"No," he admitted ruefully, then added brightly, "but I make pretty good coffee. Would that do instead?"

"That would do perfectly," Micki laughed, unsuccessfully trying to smother a yawn.

Tony's apartment was on the third floor of a large, old building, kept in excellent repair. Mumbling, "Why didn't you warn me about the stairs?" Micki groaned as they trudged upward. The apartment comprised the whole of the third floor and consisted of a fair-sized bedroom, a large kitchen-living room combination, and a small bathroom. The furniture was sparse, but what there was was comfortable and well chosen.

"Make yourself at home," Tony tossed casually, walking to the kitchen area. "Coffee will be ready in a few minutes, I have one of those almost instant things."

Micki sank onto the overstuffed sofa and sighed sleepily as the soft cushions seemed to envelop and cradle her tired body. Half asleep, the sound of Tony's quiet movement touched the fringes of her mind. There was the rattle of a tray being placed on the coffee table and a record dropping onto a turntable, then, as the cushion beside her depressed from Tony's weight, the voice of Bruce Springsteen came to her softly from the stereo.

"Are you asleep?" Tony's voice was low and soft and very, very close.

"Almost."

Lifting her heavy lids, Micki smiled into the light-blue eyes only inches away from her face. One arm resting on the back of the sofa, he leaned over her, his expression serious, somewhat sad.

"I'm going to kiss you, Micki," he murmured. The scent of alcohol came to her as his warm breath whispered over her face. Micki knew her own breath held the same tinge.

"I know."

His lips touched hers gently and then, with a low groan, his arm slid around her waist, his chest crushed hers, pushing her body deeper into the cushions, and his mouth became a driving force that searched hers with an urgency that held near desperation. At first, startled into stillness by the very intensity of his action, Micki lay unresponsive in his embrace. Then, her own feelings of desperation swamping her, she curled her arms around his neck, returned his kiss with equal fervor. Stretching his frame beside her, his hand moved down her back to the base of her spine, urging her body to meet his. Hope flaring that maybe this time she'd feel something, if only a tiny quick-

110

ening of desire, Micki arched her body to his, her arms tightening around his neck.

Other than the mild, pleasant sensation she usually felt when being kissed, there was nothing. No spark of excitement danced along her limbs, no fire rushed inside her veins, no longing to give herself up to sensual pleasure clouded her senses. She yearned for those sensations, longed to feel them, yet, even when Tony's hand moved over her rib cage to stroke her breasts, there was nothing. She could have wept in frustration and disappointment. Attuned as she was to those emotions, she felt them reciprocated from Tony when, with a strangled moan, he released her and flopped back against the sofa.

"It's no good, is it, darlin'?" It was posed as a question, yet it wasn't one. She answered anyway.

"No, it's no good, I'm sorry."

"It's not your fault." The sigh he emitted seemed to come from the depths of his being. "It's mine."

Leaning forward, he poured coffee into the two cups on the tray, lifted one, tasted it, then stood up abruptly.

"Better drink your coffee while it's still hot," he advised softly, walking to the window on the other side of the room.

Shifting to the edge of the sofa, Micki added milk to her coffee and sat staring at it, her eyes sad and misty.

"Goddamn!"

Tony's sharply expelled curse startled her upright, her eyelashes fluttering in bewilderment.

"Tony?"

Her soft entreaty brought his body around to face her, a small, apologetic smile on his lips.

"I'm sorry, Micki." Tony's lips twisted. "But I was hoping, no praying, that something would ignite between us. It would have been perfect, we're so compatible. We can laugh and talk so easily together without strain that I thought—maybe—we could make love together as easily."

Micki frowned, and knowing she misinterpreted his words, he added hastily, "Not just sex, but love—you know." His lips twisted more harshly. "The real thing, stars and music, the whole shootin' match."

"Yes, I do know." Micki's frown deepened. "It would seem that we're suffering from the same malady. You've been hurt badly, haven't you?"

"God, yes!" Tony's softly groaned exclamation tugged at her heart. Then, as the full content of her words sank in, his eyes sharpened on her face. "You too?" At her nod he probed. "Do I know him?"

Unblinking, Micki stared at him steadily until, turning palms out, he lifted his shoulders and pleaded, "Forget I said that. Bad, was it?"

"Yes."

"I know the feeling." He laughed humorlessly. "I've been there. Hell, I'm still there."

"She didn't"—Micki paused to choose her words carefully—"care for you?"

"That's the stinger." Tony's smile hurt her. "She loved me."

"But then, why?" Micki's face wore a puzzled expression. "Tony, I don't understand."

"Neither did I." He laughed harshly, puzzling her even more. Reading her expression, he lifted his shoulders again in a weary, defeated way. "I threw it away, honey," he stated flatly. "I had it all in my hands and I threw it away."

"Tony!" Micki cried in exasperation. "You are not making any sense."

"Nothing new about that," Tony sighed. "I haven't made much sense for some time now." Tilting his head, he asked quizzically, "Was I always stupid, Micki?"

"Tony!" Micki begged. "Will you stop wallowing in self-pity and explain?"

"Am I doing that?" he asked, startled, then he smiled.

"Yes, I guess I am. Sorry, hon. Are you sure you want to hear it?"

Micki nodded emphatically. "Of course. We're friends, aren't we?"

"Yes, friends." Tony's smile softened. "Okay, friend, you asked for it." Drawing a deep breath, he began. "I met her in Atlantic City. She's a supper-club singer." At the slight rise of Micki's eyebrows, his hand sliced through the air dismissively. "Oh, she had no great ambitions, no burning drive to be a star or anything. But she has an appealingly soft voice, perfect for the supper clubs, and it was a way for her to earn a good living. She comes from upstate New York and she arrived in Atlantic City via New York City." He paused and his smile turned whimsical. "We met—introduced ourselves—at a blackjack table."

"She's a gambler?" Micki exclaimed.

"Lord, no!" Tony laughed, then sobered. "Even though she gambled, and lost, on me."

"But how?" Micki cried. "Tony, *will* you explain?"

"All she wanted was marriage, children, and believe it or not, she wanted me for their father."

"You didn't want to get married?" The idea didn't surprise Micki. Many young men shied away from that total commitment.

"Hell, yes," he disabused her at once. "I wanted that more than anything in the world. But, Micki, she was so lovely and I had so damned little to offer her."

"Ah, Tony—" Micki began, but Tony's self-derisive chuckle cut her off.

"That's exactly what she said. In exactly that tone of voice. But, you see, I wanted to have everything perfect for her. I wanted to wait until I could give her a home and all the nice things that go in it." He smiled ruefully. "She didn't want to wait, told me she'd enjoy working with me to get the things we'd need." He drew a deep breath, went

113

on slowly, painfully. "I wouldn't listen, wouldn't even consider it."

"But, Tony, most young couples work together to set themselves up." Micki's face revealed her astonished reaction to his words.

"I know, I know, but—" He paused to wet his lips. "Micki, you know me, I'm great in the light moments, like earlier this evening, but when it comes to the heavy stuff, well, I freeze up. And with her it was even worse. I wanted her so much, yet I was almost afraid to touch her. I didn't merely love her, I put her on a pedestal, literally adored her. I—"

He turned away from her, his shoulders slumping, and Micki's heart ached for him all over again. When he turned back to her, his face was pale.

"She wrote me a letter." His soft tone betrayed the strain he was feeling. "Told me a friend she used to date had come down to A.C. to see the casinos and had looked her up. He asked her to marry him." Tony grimaced, but continued. "She said she couldn't wait anymore, so she was going back home with him, was going to accept his proposal." Suddenly his eyes shot blue sparks and his fingers raked his hair roughly. "I should have dragged her off the pedestal and into my bed. That's what I meant when I said I threw it away."

Micki sat staring at him long moments before, rising quickly, she walked around the sofa, her mind working at what it was about his narration that bothered her.

"Did she love you, Tony?" she finally asked.

"Yes," he answered at once. "I'd bet everything I own on that, Micki."

"Oh, Tony!" she exclaimed impatiently. "Did she take your brain with her when she left?"

"What do you mean?" he bristled.

She ignored his question to ask one of her own. "How long ago did she leave?"

"Two months, one week, and four days ago. Why?"

"Oh, for heaven's sake," she groaned. "Tony, you don't need a friend, you need a keeper. Didn't it ever occur to you she might be trying to get you off dead center?"

"In what way?" he snapped.

"Probably the second oldest way there is," she snapped back. "You made sure she couldn't use the first. She took a powder, took off, leaving a letter designed to make you jealous. You, dumbhead, were supposed to go after her."

"Do you really think so?" he asked hopefully.

"Is she married?" Again Micki brushed off his question to pose one of her own.

"I don't know."

"Why don't you?"

"For God's sake, Micki, you sound like a trial lawyer," Tony growled. "How would I know?"

"Men!" Micki's eyes lifted as if beseeching help from above. "Do you know what town she comes from? Her parents' name?"

"Well, of course." He sounded almost angry. "But what has th—"

"Call them, ask them," Micki cut in sarcastically. "They very likely know if their daughter has gotten married."

"Just like that?" Tony snapped his fingers. "Just call and ask? Come on, honey, I can't do that."

"Why not?" Micki nearly shouted in her exasperation with him. "What's so unusual about a friend calling to find out if a proposed marriage came off? A friend might want to be sure before sending a wedding gift."

Tony's eyes grew bright, then dimmed again. "What do I do if she answers the phone?"

"Ask her, you leadbrain," Micki chided. "And if the answer is no, then coax, plead, beg her to come back to you. Promise her anything, but—" she paused, her eyes twinkling. "Give her yourself, your love."

In a few long strides, Tony crossed the room, caught her

to him and hugged her fiercely before releasing her to gaze fondly into her eyes.

"You're wonderful," he said clearly. "I'll do it. Oh, baby, the guy that let you get away had to be completely crazy."

Micki winced, as much from the name *baby* as the rest of his words. Tony was instantly contrite.

"Oh, Micki, I'm sorry. What happened? Don't tell me he acted as stupid as I did?"

"No," Micki shook her head, her gentle tone robbing the denial of its sting. "He didn't put me on a pedestal." Her tone went rough. "In fact he treated me like a silly fool, called me a youngster, a juvenile." Feeling her cheeks flush, she dropped her eyes. "And he didn't have to drag me into his bed, I practically jumped into it."

"I know what it cost you to say that, honey." Tony's hand caressed her hot face. "But what happened? What went wrong?"

"I found out, after it was too late, that he was using me." Biting her lip, she lifted overbright eyes to his. "I was a very willing, convenient plaything for a weekend."

"He told you that?" Tony demanded, outraged.

"No, of course not," Micki sighed. "But the way I found out, well, it left no doubt at all as to his intentions. Oh, I'm sure he would have been willing to fit me into his schedule every now and then, as long as I didn't become difficult—or boring."

"Micki, stop." Tony's eyes were anxious, his tone concerned.

"Don't worry, Tony," Micki shook her head at him. "It all happened a long time ago. I'm fine now, really."

"Oh, sure." His tone called her a liar. "That's why you tried so hard to work up a response to me a while ago. The experience shattered you so badly you're still trying to put the pieces together." His eyes grew soft. "I can see why it would. If you know me, I know you as well. I was around, I saw how fiercely you guarded your innocence.

116

For you to give it up so willingly, you would have to be very much in love. And it still hurts, doesn't it?"

"Yes," Micki whispered.

He gazed at her silently several seconds, then his eyes narrowed in thought.

"You said it all happened a long time ago." He hesitated before probing. "Was it that time six years ago, right before you went back to college, when you called me and begged me to say yes if anyone asked if we were seeing each other regularly?"

"Yes," Micki admitted with an apologetic smile. "I'm sorry, Tony, but I'm afraid I used your name a lot at that time. I literally hid behind it."

"Sorry? Now who's being a leadbrain?" he scolded. "You may hide behind my name, or me, anytime the need arises. Now come on, it's late, I'd better get you home."

When he stopped the car in front of her house, he kissed her gently on the mouth and whispered, "If things go right, I'll send you an invitation. Okay?"

"You'd better," Micki warned.

"A promise," he vowed. "And, Micki, toss off that load of guilt and shame you've been toting."

"Yes, Tony," Micki promised meekly.

CHAPTER 7

As she slipped into bed, Micki prayed her hunch about Tony's girl had been right. She was almost sure it was, as it was exactly the sort of thing she might do in the same situation. Anxious for him, wanting to see him happy, she hoped it would not be long before, keeping his promise, he sent her an invitation to his wedding.

As to her promise to him, there was no need to worry about that, simply because she never had felt guilty or ashamed. At first, sure she should have them, she'd wondered about her lack of those feelings. The searing pain, the disappointment, the anger she'd had, hadn't had the power to change what had been a joyous experience into anything else. She'd discovered sheer delight, an exquisite Eden in Wolf's arms, and nothing that happened after that had been able to erase it from her mind.

What disturbed her was her inability to find that Eden in any other man's embrace. It was not a man's mouth that ignited the spark, but Wolf's mouth. It was not a man's hands that fanned the flame, but Wolf's hands. And it was not a man's body that could consume her in the blaze, but Wolf's body. With sad defeat, Micki faced the possibility that no other man but Wolf held the key that could unlock her emotions.

What do I do in that case? Micki wondered sleepily. Marry another man, any other man—Darrel—and act out a part the rest of my life? The thought sent a shudder down her spine and her last coherent thought was *I must call Darrel.*

It was mid-morning before Micki woke. Fuzzy minded, heavy lidded, she stumbled down the stairs and into the kitchen. Her father paused in the act of pouring a cup of coffee to give her a grin devoid of any sign of sympathy.

"Hangover?" he chirped brightly.

"No," Micki denied honestly. "But I do feel like a washout. I think I'll just loaf around the house today if I want to be in decent shape to start my job tomorrow."

"Sound thinking," Bruce intoned. "By the way, you had two phone calls last night, Wolf Renninger and a Darrel Baxter."

"Wolf?" Micki pounced on the name. "What did he want?"

Bruce shot her a sharp glance before lifting his shoulders in an I-don't-know shrug. "You'll have to ask Regina, she took the calls." Heading for the doorway Micki had just come through, he added, "If anyone wants me, I'll be on the front porch reading the paper."

Micki itched with the desire to go in search of Regina but deciding to be prudent, she poured herself a small glass of juice and a cup of coffee, dropped a slice of bread into the toaster, and sat down to wait for Regina to find her. She didn't have long to wait. Regina came into the kitchen as Micki was finishing her toast and starting on her second cup of coffee.

"Good morning, Micki," Regina greeted quietly. "Did you have a good time last night?"

"Yes, thank you," Micki answered warily, studying her stepmother's face for maliciousness. Finding none, she blurted, "I hear I had some calls last night."

120

"Yes," Regina nodded. "A young man named Darrel Baxter called soon after you left, and a short time later Wolf called."

"What did they want?" Micki asked quickly.

"To speak to you, of course," Regina replied smoothly.

"What did you, tell them?" Micki demanded sharply.

"Really, Micki." Regina's eyes flew wide at Micki's tone. "What could I tell them? I informed them both that you were out for the evening with Tony Menella. You were, weren't you?"

"Yes, yes, of course," Micki sighed contritely. "I'm sorry, Regina. I got in very late and I'm irritable this morning."

"I've experienced the feeling," Regina smiled. "Oh, yes, Mr. Baxter said he'd call sometime today."

"And Wolf?" Micki was almost afraid to ask. What, she wondered, was he up to? Why had he called when he had assured her he would not?

"Wolf said thank you very coldly and hung up," Regina replied from the counter, where she was getting herself a cup of coffee. Turning to Micki with the pot held aloft, she asked, "Can I heat yours up?"

"Yes, please."

Micki brought the cup to her lips, gulped most of the lukewarm brew down her suddenly parched throat, then handed the cup to Regina. After refilling the cup, she carried both cups to the table and sat down on the chair opposite Micki.

"Micki." Regina's tone held confusion. "What's going on?"

"Nothing's going on," Micki returned quickly. "I don't know what you mean by going on."

"You know perfectly well what I mean," Regina sighed. "The day you came home you absolutely refused to discuss Wolf Renninger. In fact you would not allow me to speak that person's name. Since then he has called here several times and you have seen him at least once that I know of. Last night Wolf's tone was not only cold, it was"—Regina hesitated, as if searching for the exact word —"proprietorial." Having found the word, she placed hard emphasis on it before going on. "I don't like feeling in the middle, while still in the dark."

When she paused for breath, Micki seized the opportunity to declare flatly, "He has no right to sound proprietorial."

"Right or not, he did," Regina retorted. "Which leads me to suspect he will be calling again. Now don't you think it's time we talked frankly about what happened six years ago and clear up that mess once and for all?"

"No!"

The chair scraped the floor and nearly toppled over as Micki jumped up. She was at the doorway when Regina's voice, sounding both tired and impatient, stopped her.

"Micki, you don't understand," Regina argued. "There are things you must know. Things about Wolf and—"

"I don't want to hear it," Micki cried, rushing through the doorway. "And I won't listen."

"For heaven's sake, Micki," Regina called after her. "This is ridiculous."

"So, okay," Micki shot back as she swung around the banister and started up the stairs, unaware of her father standing in the front doorway holding the screen door open. "I'm ridiculous."

"What in the— Micki?" Bruce's voice was sharp with concern. "What's all the shouting about? I doubt any of the neighbors missed a word."

"I'm sorry, Dad, but I can't—I won't—" Micki paused at the growing look of confusion and alarm on his face. "Oh, hell," she sighed, running up the stairs.

"Micki!" Bruce called after her, then called sharply, "Regina!"

Micki didn't wait to hear any more. She ran inside her room, slammed the door, and leaned against it, breathing heavily and fighting tears. Oh, why did Regina persist in

122

tormenting her? If she really wanted a smoother relationship between them, why didn't she let the subject drop?

Still tired from her physical and emotional exertions of the night before, Micki's thoughts tumbled, none too rationally. Were Regina and Wolf still seeing each other behind her father's back? But if they were, why had Wolf insisted she go out with him? Wasn't one woman at a time enough for him? *Damn Regina,* Micki silently cursed her, *if she hurts Dad again I'll* . . . Not knowing exactly what she'd do, Micki's fury turned to Wolf. Why was he doing this? And why, after stating so flatly that he would not call her again, had he called last night? Were Regina and Wolf working together to drive her away? That thought brought her up short.

"Please, no."

Moving her head back and forth against the smoothly finished door, Micki wasn't even aware that she'd whispered the words aloud. The very possibility of her reasoning being correct tightened a band of pain around her head. If it was true, if their affair was still going on, she, simply by being her father's daughter, and being in the house, was a definite threat to them.

Her breathing suddenly constricted, Micki stumbled across the room and dropped onto the bed. Six years ago she had thought the intensity of the pain she suffered at the image of Wolf and Regina entwined together, exactly as she and Wolf had been, could not possibly be deepened. She had been wrong. The anguish she felt now far superceded what had been before.

"Goddamn you, Wolf Renninger."

The muted curse held more the sound of an animal's snarl than the lucid words from a reasoning mind. And like an animal's claws, her elegantly long, painted nails dug viciously into the rumpled bedcovers on the unmade bed.

Harsh, rasping breaths were drawn in roughly around the unreleased sobs gripping her throat. And eyelids were anchored firmly against hot tears she refused to let run free. Curled up tightly into the fetal position, Micki's slim ball of a body caused the mattress to tremble with the force of the shudders that shook through her.

Dear God, the silent plea was wrenched from the depths of her being, *I take it back, don't damn him. Just, please, please, make him go away and leave me alone before I give in to my need for him and damn my own soul in the giving. You see, God,* the chaotic thoughts run on, *I love him so terribly, and if he manages to get me alone, I don't know how long I can hold out against the urge to lose myself, my very identity, inside his arms. If you have any mercy, help me. And, if you have any justice,* she added irreverently, bitterly, *you'll give a small slap to Regina's conscience.*

By the time she finished her somewhat unorthodox prayer, Micki's sobs filled the room and her tears soaked a patch of the sheet under her face. The sound of her sobs blocked out the quiet tap on her door and a second later the click the latch made as the door was opened. Nor did she see the alarm that filled her father's eyes as they encountered her shaking form. The anxious sound of his voice told her she was no longer alone.

"Princess, what is wrong?" Bruce probed gently, bending over the bed to stretch his hand out and smooth her hair from her damp face. "What has happened to make you cry like this? Was it something Regina said or did?"

Yes, it was both those things. Micki had to bite back the words as, rolling onto her back, she shook her head and lied. "No, of course not." Swallowing down her sobs with the air she drew into her lungs, she hiccupped, then rushed on. "I'm tired. Tony and I danced for hours last night and despite what I said, I'm afraid I drank too much. After that I went to Tony's apartment with him and—"

"You did what?" Bruce's voice, sharp with sudden anger, cut across her babbling explanation. "That's why you're crying, isn't it? What did he do to you?"

"Do?" Micki asked blankly. "What do you me—?" She

stopped, stunned, as her mind caught up with his train of thought. Before she could deny his impression, he was speaking again.

"Answer me!"

Never before had Micki heard quite that harsh a tone from her father, seen such fury in his eyes. Struck momentarily speechless, Micki stared at him in wonder.

"Well, if you won't answer me"—he swung away from the bed—"maybe he will."

"What do you mean?" Micki squeaked. "What are you going to do?"

"I'm going to call him," Bruce snapped, moving toward the door. "Better still, I think I'll go see him."

"Dad, stop!" The sobs, the tears, were forgotten as Micki scrambled off the bed to run after him, clutch at his arm. "It's not what you're thinking. I swear nothing happened."

"He didn't try to make love to you?" Bruce rapped.

"Well, not really—he—" Micki floundered.

"That's what I thought." Bruce shook her arm off, continued toward the door.

"Dad, please, nothing happened."

At the frantic, pleading note in her voice, Bruce turned to look at her, his angry eyes raking her face.

"Suppose you tell me exactly what did happen."

"Tony did kiss me," Micki admitted. "But he didn't really want me." His body stiffened and again she caught his arm, explained. "Dad, Tony is crazily in love with a girl he met in Atlantic City. What he really wanted was someone to pour his heart out to."

"And that's all?"

Watching the anger drain out of his face, Micki expelled a long sigh of relief. Her father's fury was an altogether new experience for her, never having been exposed to it before. If she hadn't seen it with her own eyes, she would not have believed it. For a few seconds there, that furious man had been a stranger, not the gentle father she thought she knew. Subdued by this new facet of her father's personality, she avowed, softly, "That is absolutely all."

"All right." Although the anger had left his expression, it still edged his tone. "But what the hell possessed you to go to his apartment in the first place?"

"But why shouldn't I have gone with him?" Micki asked, genuinely puzzled.

"Why?" Bruce exclaimed. "You know full well why. You're not that naive."

"No, I'm not," Micki returned with force. "And I'm no longer a little girl. And Tony's is not the first bachelor apartment I've been in. Good grief, Dad, I'm twenty-five years old, not sixteen."

"And everyone knows twenty-five-year-old women never get attacked." Bruce's voice dripped sarcasm. "Or hurt. That only happens to sixteen-year-old girls."

"Oh, Dad," Micki sighed. "I'm fully aware of what goes on out there in the big bad world, but I can't hide myself behind locked doors, or wrap myself in cotton."

"No, you can't," he agreed, then qualified, "but you don't have to invite trouble or go looking for it either."

Knowing there was no way she could win, but unwilling to give in, Micki insisted, "I don't go looking—"

"Micki," Regina's call ended the argument. "You're wanted on the phone."

Casting a rueful glance at her father, Micki left the room. Who, she wondered in amazement, would have believed he'd react like that. And what in the world would he have done had he ever found out about the weekend she'd spent with Wolf? A shudder rippling through her, she started down the stairs only to stop suddenly, her breath catching in her throat. Could that be Wolf on the phone now? Slowly, her steps lagging, Micki descended the stairs, went into the living room, and picked up the receiver.

"Hello?"

"Micki?"

The well-modulated sound of Darrel's voice left Micki weak with relief and, contrarily, a bit disappointed.

"Yes, Darrel. How are you? I was planning to call you this afternoon."

"Where?"

His query stopped her for a moment. What did he mean, where?

"At your apartment, of course," she finally answered. "Where else would I call?"

"Since yesterday afternoon"—Darrel's voice held a smile—"my mother's summer place in Cape May."

"You're calling from Cape May now?"

"Isn't that what I just said?" He laughed indulgently. "I'm glad I finally found you at home." No laughter or even a tinge of a smile now. "Did you have a good time last night?"

Something—was it censure—about his tone annoyed her, so she answered oversweetly. "Yes, I had a wonderful time." Well, she had, for the most part anyway. Her answer met a short silence. When he spoke again, his tone conveyed a worried mixture of anger and hesitation.

"How—nice." Again there was a tiny silence. "Micki, mother's having a small dinner party this evening and she expressly asked me to bring you. Will you come?"

Expressly? I'll bet. Micki's mouth curved wryly. She was very well aware that his mother did not consider her nearly good enough for her precious son. Should she go? Why not? she asked herself. Mrs. Baxter would know before too long that Micki posed no threat to her plans for Darrel's future.

"I'd love to," she lied blandly. "What time should I come?"

"I was hoping you'd agree to my coming up there now," he said quickly. "Then we could have some time alone together before returning here for dinner. Also it would afford me the opportunity to meet your father and stepmother."

Don't bother, buster, you're on your way out. The outrageous thought skittered into Micki's mind, only to be swept quickly out again. Whatever was the matter with her? Why was she feeling so bitchy? It's all Wolf's fault, him and his damn phone call after telling her he wouldn't call. The fact that there was no sense at all to her reasoning didn't bother her in the least.

"Micki? Are you there?"

"Yes, yes, Darrel," Micki assured him. "I was just trying to remember if I'd made any commitments for the day." Liar. "As I can't remember any, yes, you can come up. Say, in an hour?"

"Good, I'll be there."

"How should I dress?"

"Oh, casually I'd say. See you in an hour."

After she had replaced the receiver, Micki stood staring at the instrument, the wry smile back on her lips. Oh, casually, the man said. Oh, sure. As casually as labels that read Dior or Halston and that ilk. In other words, girl, she told herself as she left the room, you had better dress casually—to the teeth.

Micki spent the entire hour on her appearance, choosing carefully everything she put on down to the shade of varnish she brushed on her nails. On opening the door for Darrel, she counted the time well spent by the expression on his face.

"You're so lovely," he said softly. He took one step, his arms reaching for her, then, realizing where he was, he stopped, placed his hands lightly on her waist and bent to kiss her cheek. "I've missed you, darling."

"And I've missed you," Micki replied, trying in vain to infuse conviction into her tone.

After making the introductions, Micki stood aside watching Darrel charm her father and Regina. No one she had ever met could be quite as charming as Darrel. Intelligent, handsome, urbane, his athletically slim body encased in perfectly tailored clothes, he was every parent's dream of a husband. By both her father's and Regina's reaction, they were not any exception.

After a two-week separation, her own reaction to him surprised her. Watching him, listening to him, she heaved a silent sigh of relief that she had decided not to marry him. He was almost too perfect. Too good-looking, too well turned out, too charming. How, she wondered, could she have ever lived up to that, or with it, twenty-four hours a day? A picture of her own jean-clad, barefoot, tousle-headed form, as she usually was when around the house, rose in her mind, and she had to fight the grin that tugged at her lips. While working, Micki always looked like she'd stepped off the cover of a high-fashion magazine. But when she was at home, well, that was a different story. To her own way of thinking she was more real when she was at home.

After they had left the house and were in his car—a custom-made black Cadillac—driving south, Micki continued with her train of thought. Studying him and the situation objectively, she was convinced that had she married him she would have lost her real self, the essence that was Micki Durrant.

With a small jolt of surprise Micki suddenly realized that Darrel had seen her only in her workday facade. What, she mused, would he think of the tomboyish Micki who could still scamper up a tree with the best of them? Or, the curves revealed by a bikini not withstanding, become joyfully covered with gritty particles as she erected a sand castle of enormous proportions? She did not have to witness his reaction to know it. Again an impish grin tugged at her lips, more successfully this time.

"What amuses you?" Darrel's tone held just a touch of the petulant child left out of a secret. Yes, indeed, she decided, Darrel would be very hard, if not impossible, for her to live with.

"Life," Micki answered, her bright-blue eyes dancing. "And its funny little twists and turns."

"I find very little amusement in twists and turns," Darrel intoned. "I like my life well planned and ordered. After we're married"—he seemed unaware of Micki's small gasp—"you'll have no more twists and turns, and I'm sure you will find life less unnerving."

Not to mention a lot less exciting, Micki thought scathingly. How was it possible, she asked herself, for a man to be so charming one minute and so pompously dull the next? She didn't even try to work out the answer to that one, as having already rejected him in her mind, she proceeded to do so in fact.

"But we're not going to be married." Although her tone was gentle, it was also flat with finality.

"Not going to be—!" The big car swerved slightly before Darrel's white-knuckled hands gripped the wheel and straightened it. "But I thought it was settled."

"I don't know why you should have thought that," Micki said quietly. "The only promise I made to you before I left Wilmington was to think about your proposal. I have, and I've reached the conclusion that it simply would not work."

"But of course it would work," he insisted. "Why wouldn't it?"

"In the first place," Micki replied calmly, "your mother does not approve of me. And—"

"You're wrong," Darrel interrupted sharply. "At least she no longer objects to the union. She has reconciled herself to the—"

"And in the second place," she cut him off forcefully, "I'm not in love with you."

"But you would learn to love me." He was actually pleading! "I could make you love me."

"No, Darrel, you could not," she assured him gently, but firmly. "Of that I am very sure."

"There is someone else?" His eyes had left the road for a moment as he asked the question. Micki's momentarily unguarded expression was all the answer he needed.

"Yes," he sighed, glancing back at the road. "I can see there is."

"I'm sorry." The words sounded inadequate, even to her own ears, yet they were all she had to offer.

"Sorry? Sorry?" His tone held an anger she'd never heard from him before. "What good is sorry? Why didn't you tell me at once? When I first asked you to marry me?" His voice died away, then came back more strongly. "Why the hell did you let me hang like that when you knew the answer was no all along?"

"But I didn't—" Micki began, then stopped, aghast at what she was admitting to him.

"You didn't know?" he finished for her. "You mean it's some man you've met within the last two weeks?"

"Yes—no!" Micki cried.

"What do you mean, yes—no?" Darrel demanded. "For God's sake, Micki, make up your mind. It's either one or the other."

Having arrived at their destination, Cape May's charmingly quaint shopping mall, Micki was allowed a few minutes to form her answer while Darrel searched out a parking space.

The second the car was motionless, he turned to face her, his expression grim.

"Well?"

"Well," Micki began slowly, "both yes and no are correct." At his look of disbelief, she hurried on. "Yes, really, Darrel." Micki hesitated, wet her lips, then admitted, "I met, and fell in love with, him some years ago. I was very young." Again she moistened her dry lips, looked in every direction but his. "I had hoped, was sure, that it was all over." She paused to draw breath and he took the opportunity to question her.

"That's why you really came home, wasn't it?" His voice was heavy with accusation. "To see him."

"No, it was not," Micki denied. "I never expected to see

131

him again. When I ran into him, purely by accident, I—I realized nothing had changed for me."

"For you?" Listening carefully, Darrel had caught the inflection in her last two words. "He doesn't love you anymore?"

"He never did." It wasn't easy but she managed to lift her head and meet his penetrating glance. "All he ever wanted was an affair. He still does."

"And you've agreed to this?" he exclaimed, astonished. No man knew better than Darrel exactly how cool and unresponsive Micki could be.

"Of course not," Micki snapped icily.

"Well then," he argued, "if there is no future for you with him, why not—" That was as far as he got before Micki trod on his words.

"I'll tell you why not. Very simply, I can't marry or sleep with one man while loving another." She smiled sadly. "I'm sorry, Darrel, but that's not my style."

"Yes, I know." Darrel's smile matched hers for sadness for several minutes before he shrugged. "I suppose, under the circumstances, dinner at mother's would not be a good idea. She was halfway expecting an announcement of our engagement." His shoulders moved again. "I'll call her and tell her we can't make it, and face the questions tomorrow." The sadness left his smile, replaced by all the charm he was capable of. "You will have dinner with me, won't you?"

"No pressure?" Micki asked warily.

"No pressure," he vowed. "I may not know you all that long, but I know you well enough to be sure no amount of pressure would change your mind."

Micki had a sudden urge to cry. The words *no amount of pressure* brought home to her more than anything else how very vulnerable she was. It would, she knew, take very little pressure from Wolf to turn her into a pliant, shivering love slave. *How very little we know each other,* she thought sadly. She was considered very strong-willed and near frigid by most, if not all, of her friends. What would Darrel's reaction be, she wondered, if he were exposed to a tenth of the passion that had consumed her while on Wolf's boat? A conjured picture of Darrel's shocked visage exchanged the hovering tears for a fleeting smile.

"What are you thinking?" he probed. "You're so quiet, and for a second there I wasn't sure if you were going to laugh or cry."

"For a second there, I wasn't sure either," Micki laughed softly. "I wanted to cry for what might have been. Darrel, would you do something for me?"

"Of course," he answered at once. "Anything. What is it?"

"Would you buy me a sandwich?" Her eyes bright with the recent moisture teased impishly. "I just realized I haven't eaten for hours and I'm starving."

Up until then the car's engine, which he'd left on to run the air-conditioner, had purred softly. As he turned to shut off the engine, he shook his head ruefully.

"You're unbelievable, Micki." As if against his will, he smiled. "To use a very trite phrase, how can you think of food at a time like this?" His smile deepened and grew into a grin. "But now that you mention it, I could eat a sandwich myself."

They left the cool confines of the car to brave the fierce assault from the sun and the waves of heat rising from the sidewalk. Strolling along the perimeter of the shopping mall, they came upon a restaurant with a low-walled patio. On the patio were a half dozen umbrella-shaded tables surrounded by wooden deck chairs. Only two of the tables were occupied, and the waitress, looking somewhat forlorn, cast them a hopeful look.

"What do you think?" Darrel laughed softly. "The patio? Or would you prefer the air-conditioned dining room?"

"Oh, the patio," Micki grinned. "I don't think I have the courage to bypass that waitress."

Chatting pleasantly, the waitress took their orders of grilled cheese and bacon sandwiches and iced tea before reluctantly disappearing through a door at the far end of the patio.

"Well," Darrel sighed, pushing back his chair. "I may as well find a phone, face the music, and get it over with. I'll be back in a minute, if I'm lucky."

"Take your time, I'll be fine." Micki waved him away. "Please convey my regrets to your mother." A low grunt was the only reply she received.

A mild breeze ruffling her hair, Micki leaned back in the chair and let her gaze roam over the surrounding area. Moving lazily, her eyes passed a glare of red, then, a soft gasp escaping her parted lips, her eyes honed in on the flame-colored car.

With something akin to panic, Micki watched as the sports car was maneuvered into a small parking space. Even without a good view of the man behind the wheel, Micki knew who was driving that brazenly painted, rich man's toy. She very seriously doubted there were two cars like that on the whole of the south Jersey coast.

A growing ache gripping her throat, Micki watched as Wolf stepped out of the car, walked around to the other side to assist his passenger in alighting. Hating herself, yet unable to tear her eyes away, Micki studied the woman as she stepped onto the street and straightened up. At that distance Micki could only get an impression of the woman. That impression was tall, willowy, her platinum hair gleaming in the sunlight, her face partially concealed by overlarge sunglasses, her teeth flashing whitely in a crimson mouth.

"Here's your tea, miss." The waitress's lilting voice drew Micki's attention. "Your sandwiches will be along in a moment."

"Thank you, I need that," Micki croaked. "I'm parched."

Sipping gratefully at the cold drink, Micki kept her eyes firmly on the glass, determined not to look at him again. An instant later, unable to stop herself, she lifted her head and froze, the ache in her throat culling forth a corresponding one in her chest. Fighting a desire to jump up and run, she watched as the couple walked in a direct line toward her. Aware that as yet, due to the obviously deep conversation they were engaged in, Wolf had not spotted her, Micki had to force herself to stay in her chair.

Let him pass by without seeing me, please, Micki begged silently. Apparently it was not her day with the deity, for at that moment Wolf turned from the woman and saw Micki. His step quickened and his eyes widened, then, looking beyond her, narrowed.

"God!" Darrel's harassed voice reached her an instant before he slipped into the chair beside her. "My mother should have gone into law, she would have made a fantastic D.A."

Tearing her gaze from the silvery eyes fastened on her, Micki stammered, "Bad, was it?"

"Rock bottom," he groaned. "She had more questions than an end-of-term exam." Raising his glass, Darrel took a long swallow. "Oh, that's good, even though I'm sorry now I didn't order something stronger."

Micki barely heard him. An odd, eerie feeling cloaking her, she knew without looking that Wolf and the tall woman had entered the patio. She didn't even blink when his low voice drew her head around.

"Hello, Micki."

Blue eyes locked with silver and for one mad second Micki was tempted to ignore him. The sure knowledge that in no way would Wolf allow her to get away with it chased temptation out of her mind.

"Hello, Wolf," Micki replied with amazing coolness. "Cape May seems to be a very popular place today."

"Yes, doesn't it." Until that minute his eyes had refused to release hers, now they swung pointedly to Darrel, who had risen at Wolf's greeting.

"Darrel Baxter," Micki smiled painfully. "Wolf Renninger and—" The breath died in her throat as, shifting her gaze, Micki got a good look at the woman by Wolf's side. Her hair was not platinum, but a beautiful true silver and, although she was still strikingly lovely, she appeared to be somewhere in her middle sixties.

"Mrs. Bianca Perriot," Wolf finished for her. "Bianca —Miss Micki Durrant and Mr. Darrel Baxter."

Returning the woman's enchanting smile, Micki extended her hand, felt her fingers grasped in a firm handshake at the same time the two men performed the same act.

"Micki." Bianca's voice was every bit as enchanting as her smile. "What a delightful name. Is it a given name or a nickname?"

"Given," Micki answered softly. "In honor of my Irish grandfather, who by all accounts, was a real Mick."

Bianca's laughter tinkled on the air like the sound of tiny bells before, turning to Darrel, she placed her hand in his and queried, "Baxter? Are you by any chance related to Martha Baxter?"

"My mother." Darrel's tone betrayed his surprise. "You're acquainted with her?"

"I know her very well. I knew your father also." Once again that enchanting smile came to her lips. "My late husband was as avid a golfer as your father was. They played together quite often, leaving your mother and me to amuse ourselves at the clubhouse."

During this exchange, though Micki determinedly kept her attention centered on Bianca Perriot's animated face, she was uncomfortably aware of Wolf's eyes devouring her. When Darrel spoke again, his words went through her like a blast of arctic air.

"Were you and Mr. Renninger planning to have some-

136

thing to eat here?'' At her assenting nod, Darrel asked, "Then won't you join us? We'd love the company, wouldn't we, Micki?''

What could she possibly say? Her eyes wide with shock, she swung her gaze to Wolf. The glittery spark that blended with the silver told her she'd get no assistance from him. He was enjoying her discomfort. Biting back a moan, she curved her lips in a parody of a smile and lied.

"Yes, of course, we'd love to have you join us."

CHAPTER 8

Uncomfortable and uneasy, Micki stole another glance at Wolf as he seated Bianca. At the same moment his glance shifted to her, his eyes glittering wickedly.

"All set to start the new job tomorrow, Micki?"

The lazily drawled question turned her unease into dismay. With those few words Wolf had managed to convey a familiarity between them to Darrel and Bianca. Pretending she didn't notice Darrel's startled reaction, Micki glared daggers at Wolf, her lips straining to keep her smile in place.

"Yes," she answered softly. "I've enjoyed my vacation, but I'm ready to go back to work."

"Micki is a buyer for Something Different boutiques," Wolf informed Bianca, adding to the familiarity. "She has just been transferred to the Atlantic City store."

"Oh! But—" Bianca began, her face mirroring confusion.

"Promoted."

The sharp word Darrel flung at Wolf cut across Bianca's quiet voice. For several seconds his eyes blazed a challenge at Wolf, then, as if suddenly realizing his rudeness, he smiled at Bianca and murmured, "I'm sorry I

139

interrupted. Micki was promoted." His eyes flashed to Wolf. "Not transferred."

"Yes, of course." Wolf's cold as steel eyes contradicted his smooth tone. "I knew that."

Feeling caught in their crossfire and growing angry at the childish way they were squaring off at each other, Micki snapped, "Transferred, promoted, what difference does it make?"

Without waiting for a reply from either of them, Micki continued, "Either way, I begin tomorrow and I'm eager to start. Now," she finished strongly, "can we drop the subject?"

Bianca's puzzled expression slowly changed to one of amusement as her eyes shifted from one to the other of them. Her lips twitching, she soothed, "Micki's right, it is unimportant and—oh, good, here's our waitress."

The tension around the table eased with the arrival of the waitress, even though Micki felt the angry stiffness in Darrel when his arm brushed hers as he drew his chair closer to the table.

The waitress placed the delicious-looking, open-face sandwiches in front of Micki and Darrel, whipped two menus out from under her arm, and offering them to Bianca and Wolf, chirped, "Can I get you folks something to drink?"

"I don't need that." Wolf waved the menu away. "I'll have a Reuben and a beer."

"And," Bianca smiled, "as those sandwiches look good enough to eat, I'll have one of those and a glass of Chablis."

"You can bring me a beer too," Darrel inserted as the waitress moved to turn away. "Micki?"

"Another iced tea." Micki smiled faintly at the woman before, in a chiding way that left little doubt she was reminding Darrel of his manners, she emphasized, "Please."

At any other time Micki would have enjoyed being in

Bianca's company, even though the exact relationship between the attractive woman and Wolf tormented her more than she cared to admit to herself. Being a permanent year-round resident of Cape May, Bianca was a fund of information on the town's history. Had it not been for her enlightening conversation, the atmosphere around the table would have been much more uncomfortable.

Even so Micki could hardly wait until the food had been consumed and the check was presented. Sighing with relief, Micki smiled brightly at the waitress when she placed the check on the table. The smile turned to a silent groan as hostilities were resumed between Wolf and Darrel.

"I'll take care of that."

Moving swiftly, Wolf's hand grabbed the check out from under Darrel's.

"But I invited you to join us." Darrel's angry glance clashed with glinting silver.

"But we intruded on your, er, privacy." Hard finality laced Wolf's tone as, turning away check in hand, he strode toward the building's entrance.

Finally they were back in the car heading for Ocean City.

"He's the man, isn't he?" Darrel shot the question at her savagely after some fifteen minutes of total silence. The suddenness of his attack startled Micki out of the blue funk she'd drifted into.

"W-what man?" she hedged.

"You know damned well what man," he growled frustratedly. "The bastard who's willing to fit you into his schedule now and then."

"Darrel, please."

"Please, hell," he snorted. "Do you have any idea how it makes me feel, knowing you turned me down for a man like that? Oh, I grant you," he sneered, "he's got the kind of looks that attract the females. Of all ages apparently. As lovely and charming as Bianca Perriot is, the fact remains she is old enough to be his mother."

141

"Darrel." Micki's tone was sharp with admonishment. "Don't jump to conclusions. You don't know—"

"Don't kid yourself," Darrel interrupted jeeringly. "A man like Wolf—how apt, that name—doesn't waste his time on any woman unless she's coming across."

"Darrel!" Micki's shocked exclamation revealed the depth of pain his words had inflicted.

"Darrel what?" Unrepentant, he continued to fling words at her like blows. "Face the facts, Micki, he's a user and age means nothing. What does he do to earn a living?"

"I . . ." Micki paused, wet her lips, then admitted, "I don't know."

"I thought not." He shot a pitying glance at her and went on mercilessly. "I'll tell you what I think he does. I think the polite term is paid escort but, to call a spade a spade, I think he's a stud for hire."

"Be quiet!" Micki shouted angrily. "Don't you dare say another word. Even if what you say is true, it is none of your business." Her voice dwindling to a soft sigh, she added, "Or mine either."

They covered the remaining miles to her home in uneasy silence. The minute he stopped the car in front of the house, Micki flung the door open and ran out.

"Micki, wait," Darrel pleaded. "I'm sorry, I—"

"I don't want to talk about it," Micki snapped coldly.

"May I call you later in the week?" he called after her.

"No," Micki flung over her shoulder. "Or ever again."

"Micki!"

Walking quickly, she went into the house and closed the door on the sound of his voice. Her breath coming in gasps, Micki ran up the stairs and into her room. Taking short, agitated steps, she paced her room, around the bed to the window, then, turning sharply, back to the door again.

It wasn't true, she assured herself. What Darrel said wasn't true, it couldn't be, could it? No, of course it couldn't be. But what did he do for a living? What kind

142

of job was it that paid enough to afford him the expensive clothes he wore, that boat and—she winced—that fantastic car. How much did a car like that cost anyway? More bucks than an ordinary job paid, of that she was sure. And the slacks and shirt he was wearing today! Micki's trained eyes had told her they were hand tailored and had very probably cost him more than she earned in a month. And Bianca Perriot's simple little summer frock had practically screamed the words *created in Paris*. Was she very wealthy? Very, very likely, Micki decided. And the suspicious little thought crept into her mind: Had Bianca's still-smooth, diamond-bedecked slim hand written the check that had paid for Wolf's clothes?

Aghast at herself, Micki tore out of her room and along the hall to the stairs, running from her thoughts. It didn't work; her thoughts followed her. A note on the kitchen table informed her that her father and Regina had gone out for dinner. Alone, the quiet of the house pressing in on her, she curled up in a corner of the sofa, paperback in hand, in a vain attempt to lose herself.

She was reading a paragraph for the third time when the phone rang. Silently apologizing to the author, she put the book down and lifted the receiver.

"Hello?"

"Micki?" Tony's exuberant voice attacked her eardrum. "I couldn't wait to send you an invitation, I had to call you."

"You called her?" Micki exclaimed. "You talked to her?"

"I'm with her now," Tony laughed. "I didn't sleep at all last night. I kept thinking about what you said, asking myself should I, shouldn't I? Anyway, I called her first thing this morning and damned if you weren't right. Not only is she not married, or getting married—except to me—there was no ex-boyfriend at all." His laughter this time held a rueful note, and Micki could imagine him shaking his head. "I'll tell you, friend, it's a good thing I spilled my guts out to you last night; she was about ready to give up on me."

"After waiting this long?" Micki chided. "I somehow doubt that."

"Yes, well, she's not waiting any longer," Tony said determinedly. "And neither am I. We're getting married next Saturday and we want you to come. Can you make it, Micki?"

The anxious note that had crept into Tony's voice brought a rush of tears to Micki's eyes. "Can birds fly?" she shot back at him with a shaky laugh. "Just tell me what time, where, and give me directions and I'll be there with wedding bells on."

"If you'd want to, you could fly into Albany and I could meet the plane," he suggested. "Save you all that driving."

"You're on," Micki agreed. "I'll check into flight schedules tomorrow. Suppose you call me sometime midweek and I'll let you know what time."

"Will do. And Micki?" Tony's voice went rough with emotion. "We both thank you."

"You're both welcome," she whispered. Then she added, "Tony, does she have a name?"

"Shirley," Tony laughed. "Don't you love it?"

After she'd replaced the receiver, Micki went back to the sofa, a small smile curving her lips. Tony Menella getting married! Unbelievable. Memories rushed over her, and caught up in the flow, the tormenting suspicions about Wolf were pushed to the back of her mind.

The first thing that greeted Micki when she walked into the shop Monday morning was an announcement. Georgine, her large, dark eyes bright with excitement, was fairly twitching with news.

"I've been transferred."

"Transferred?" Micki cried. "Where? When?"

"The boss was in the day after you were here," Geor-

144

gine laughed. "Told me they were opening a new store, asked me if I'd like to manage it."

"Manage? Georgine that's wonderful," Micki enthused.

"That's what I thought," she drawled. "Then, when he told me where the store is he asked if I still wanted it." Her dark eyes rolled expressively. "I asked him if he'd like my eye teeth." Her beautiful face was drawn into a sober cast and her voice rasped deeply. " 'No, thank you,' the man said, 'I've got a good set of fangs of my own.' "

The word *fangs* sent a picture of Wolf flashing into Micki's mind, and shaking her head impatiently, she pleaded, "Georgine, will you tell me where the store is?"

Georgine mentioned a large hotel chain, then said casually, "The one in Honolulu."

"Honolulu?" Micki repeated in an awed tone, then, much louder, "Honolulu?"

Jennell's soft laughter drifted to her from across the width of the shop, where both she and Lucy had stood watching Micki's reaction to the news. Then she drawled huskily, "Isn't it a shame? I mean, some poor girls have no luck at all. First Georgine can't find a man, now she gets shipped almost to the end of the earth—poor thing."

Georgine's excitement infected them all and Micki's first week at the store flew by without a hitch. Even her plans for attending Tony and Shirley's wedding went smoothly. Plans were also made by Micki, Jennell, and Lucy to take Georgine for dinner on Friday night, as she was leaving for Honolulu on Monday.

When she learned Micki was flying to Albany Saturday morning, Jennell suggested she pack a valise, bring it with her to the shop Friday, and spend the weekend at her apartment.

"I'll drive you to the airport Saturday morning and pick you up again Saturday night," Jennell said. "That way you won't have to leave your car at the airport."

All Micki's arguments about not wanting to put Jennell

out ended up against a stone wall. Jennell was determined and Micki finally, laughingly, gave in.

Friday night was pure fun. After a wildly expensive dinner they went bar hopping, having decided there was safety in numbers, flirting madly and dancing until Micki thought she'd drop.

Saturday morning, still half asleep, Micki waved goodbye to an equally sleepy Jennell, boarded the plane, and promptly fell asleep, dead to the world until the plane touched down in Albany. A grinning Tony woke her completely with a bear hug and resounding kiss on the mouth.

"What are you up to?" Micki grinned back at him when he released her.

"Oh, five-eleven, et cetera," Tony chirped. "I wanted to bring Shirl with me to meet you, but I'm not allowed to see the bride before the ceremony." His grin flashed again. "So come on, friend. You and I are going to have some lunch and you can hold my hand between now and then. Maybe you can even prevent the nervous fit I feel coming on."

Micki's first glimpse of Shirley was just before the ceremony and with that quick look she knew why Tony had put the young woman on a pedestal and had hesitated about making love to her. Small, fragile Shirley had the face of a modern-day Madonna. Her own breath catching in her throat, Micki could well imagine the impact Shirley had on a supper-club crowd.

Although the ceremony was brief, it was beautiful and moving, and as Micki left the small church, she had to dab quickly at her eyes to blot the tears.

At the champagne supper given by the bride's parents, Micki discovered the girl behind the breathtaking face was not only very nice, but intelligent and quick-witted as well. When they saw her off at the airport, Micki kissed Shirl on the cheek and whispered, "I know you'll be very happy." Then loud enough for Tony to hear, "Keep this clown in line, won't you?"

"This clown wants a kiss too," Tony retorted, repeating his bear hug performance of that morning.

Tears in her eyes, Micki kissed him, warned him he'd better take damned good care of her new friend, then walked away from them with the advice they get on with the honeymoon and let her sniffle in peace.

Jennell was waiting as promised and had to hear all the wedding details on the way back to her apartment. Micki had all day Sunday to rest in the apartment by herself, as Jennell decided to do her boyfriend a favor and spend the day—and night—with him.

The nighttime part Micki found out about when Jennell telephoned the apartment around nine.

"Would you be all right on your own tonight, honey?" Jennell drawled the question hesitantly.

"Of course," Micki said at once. "Why?"

"Well, this deliciously bad man wants me to stay with him tonight, but I told him I'd have to confer with you first."

"Would you like to stay?" Micki asked devilishly.

"Is the ocean salty?" Jennell laid the drawl on thickly.

"Then stay," Micki laughed. "And Jennell."

"Yes, sugar?"

"Be good."

"Are you crazy?" Jennell purred. "I'll be terrific."

Laughing softly, Micki replaced the receiver, then went still as a strange thought struck her. Why was it, she wondered, that she was so liberal-minded about her friends' sleeping arrangements and so rigid about her own? She knew, because Jennell had been open and frank, that this "deliciously bad" man was not the first Jennell had slept with, yet she in no way thought of Jennell as promiscuous.

In fact, now that she gave it some thought, Micki could not come up with one name out of all her female friends who had not unashamedly admitted to sleeping with their current man. Why did she have to be odd woman out? Were her moral guidelines too narrow? Micki had never thought so, but, damn, she was the one alone tonight, every night.

The questions, all with the same theme, chased each other around in her mind as she prepared for bed. As she slid between the sheets the answer, which had been demanding exposure, finally broke through her self-imposed mental barrier. Very simply, she had felt no desire or even the slightest urge to be with any man other than one Wolf Renninger. And that one man scared the hell out of her. What had Darrel called him? A user of women? From her own experience Micki was very much afraid Darrel's judgment was correct. And what scared her was the almost certain feeling that should he get his hands on her again she would revel in his using, lose herself completely, and when his use of her was over, be lost forever.

Micki's second week in the shop sped by as quickly as the first. Georgine's absence was felt in more ways than one. Not only did they miss her droll sense of humor but her help in the shop as well. A sudden spurt of business kept them all on the run, and by the end of the week had nearly wiped out their stock of marked-down merchandise.

Saturday morning, half asleep and yawning, Micki walked into the kitchen to find her father and Regina talking over their after-breakfast coffee.

"Good morning, princess," Bruce smiled gently, studying her sleepy-eyed face. "You look tired, rough week?"

Returning the greeting, Micki nodded in answer. She had seen little of them all week, as staying late after the store closed to help Jennell straighten and restock the shop, she had shared a quick meal with her before driving home. She had found the house empty every night but Monday and had been asleep before they had returned.

Now Micki smiled her thanks as Regina placed a glass

of juice and a cup of coffee on the table in front of her and murmured, "How was your week?"

"Oh, not bad," Bruce replied casually, too casually. That and the bright sheen of excitement in his eyes alerted her. "As a matter of fact we concluded that deal I was telling you about a couple of weeks ago. Do you remember?"

"Yes, I remember," Micki emphasized with a nod. "It's a very big deal?"

"Involving millions eventually," Bruce grinned. "And it's all signed and sealed and tonight we celebrate."

"I remember that also," Micki laughed before jumping up. Then she went over to her father and hugged him. "Congratulations. You've been working on this some time, haven't you?"

"A good long time," Bruce sighed, shaking his head. "With all the maneuvering and negotiating and people involved—several years." He exhaled harshly. "For a while there, when I was hospitalized, I was afraid I was out of it. But this one," he nodded at Regina, "was fantastic. She became my legs, did all the running around for me, eased the pressure. And she shares equally in the rewards. So you may extend your congratulations in her direction as well."

Stunned, Micki stared at Regina for a moment. Regina's expression, a mixture of hesitancy and hope, loosened her tongue.

"Congratulations, fantastic lady." Micki's tone, though light, held real sincerity.

"Thank you."

The two simply spoken words conveyed an equally simple message to Micki. The hostilities between them were over. Micki nodded her head sharply once, sniffed, cleared her throat, then asked overbrightly, "What time does the celebration begin and where?"

"It began right here a moment ago," Bruce answered huskily. "It will continue at another realtor's place with

149

a cold buffet lunch between one and two thirty and a clambake supper at seven. We'd like to leave here around twelve thirty, as the place is some miles inland. Can you be ready by then?"

"Yes, of course." Micki smiled, swallowing around the tightness in her throat caused by the suspicious brightness in his eyes. "How many people will be there?"

"Thirty or forty I expect." He grinned at the look of dismay that crossed her face. "Don't worry, honey, you'll know quite a few of them."

On arrival at the large country house Micki judged her father's estimate to be short by at least ten. But he had been right about one thing, she did know quite a few of the people.

Micki stayed with her father and Regina until after they had finished lunch, then she wandered off on her own to explore the extensive and beautiful grounds.

The place looked like a picture out of a magazine, and content with her own company, Micki strolled across the putting green, around the tennis courts, and onto the fringes of the pool area. Shading her eyes against the fierce glare of the sun's rays striking off the water, Micki watched a group of teenagers playing Follow the Leader off the diving board.

Continuing on, she completed her wide circling of the grounds, ending up on the other side of the house. It was another hot, humid day in a long summer that had grown monotonous with hot, humid days. As she threaded her way through the cars parked in front of the three-car garage, Micki brushed her hand over her perspiration-slick face, shivering as sweat trickled between her breasts and down her back.

Walking around the front of the house, she headed for the patio from where she'd begun her exploration. There were few people there, as most of the younger ones were either in the pool or engaged in other outdoor games and the older ones had retreated into the air-conditioned house

150

where several bridge games were in session. After unwisely gulping down two gin and tonics at the small bar that had been set up at the end of the patio, she found a lounge chair in the shade, sank onto it, and was asleep within ten minutes.

As the sun trekked its way west, it inched up Micki's body, waking her when it touched her face. Bathed in sweat, her clothes plastered to her, feeling headachy and half sick, she went to the ground floor powder room. The cool interior of the house was a shock to her overheated body, and after rinsing her face and neck, she stood long minutes resting her forehead on the cool tiles. The rattle of the doorknob jerked her upright, and leaving the room she smiled wanly at the woman waiting to enter.

"They're about ready to serve the clambake," the woman informed her as she stepped into the powder room.

The thought of food made Micki's stomach lurch. She made her way slowly back to the patio and was about to step outside when she stopped cold, her breath suddenly constricted in her chest.

Wolf, looking cool and relaxed in lightweight tan slacks and a pale blue shirt, stood at the bar talking to two men. About to retreat and find another way to the area where the tables had been set up for supper, Micki heard the one man say, "Since you're alone today, Wolf, what do you say we do a disappearing act after supper and hunt up some action?"

"No, thanks." Wolf's soft laughter sent a shiver through Micki. "When this Wolf goes on the prowl, he prowls alone."

The sickness increasing inside, Micki turned away sharply. His own words seemed to confirm Darrel's opinion of him. How could she be in love with a man like that? And what was he doing here anyway?

She was halfway across the room when her steps faltered, then stopped, her hand reaching out for something to hang on to. The room seemed to be moving around her

151

and she felt funny, almost floaty. Then her fingers were caught by a hard male hand and a sharp voice demanded, "Micki, what's wrong? Are you sick?"

"I—I feel funny." Was that watery voice hers?

"Sit down." As he spoke, Wolf guided her into a chair, lowered her head gently to her knees, muttering, "Damn, no one's around, they're all at supper."

The light-headedness passed and Micki urged, "I'm all right now. Please go back to your friends."

"Don't talk so damned dumb," Wolf snapped. "I'm taking you home."

"But—"

That's as far as she got, for scooping her into his arms, Wolf ordered, "Be quiet," and carried her out of the house. He deposited her in his car and had turned to walk around to the driver's side when she exclaimed, "Dad and Regina! They'll wonder what happened to me."

"Relax," Wolf soothed. "I'll tell them."

Within minutes he was back sliding behind the wheel. Her head resting against the seat, eyes closed, Micki heard the engine roar to life, felt the car move slowly as he drove onto the road, then with a sudden surge, the Ferrari seemed to literally fly along the highway. Afraid to open her eyes, Micki listened for the siren's wail from a patrol car all the way home.

When Wolf brought the car to a stop in front of her home, Micki stirred lethargically and murmured, "Thank you."

He didn't bother answering. He picked up her handbag and dug through it until he found her keys. Holding them up, he asked, "Which one?"

Ignoring her protests that it wasn't necessary, he helped her from the car and into the house. Once again the air-conditioned coolness went through her like a shock, and dropping into the first chair she came to, Micki closed her eyes against the renewed dizziness. She heard Wolf moving away and had to bite back a plea for him to stay.

Tears were slipping out from under her tightly closed eyes when she felt something cool and wet touch her face. Wiping gently, Wolf bathed her face and neck.

"That's good," Micki sighed. Nearly unconscious, unaware that she spoke aloud, she murmured, "I haven't felt this bad since the abortion."

The damp cloth stopped moving and stirring restlessly she pleaded, "Don't stop."

"What abortion?" There was an odd, breathless quality to Wolf's husky tone that confused her already fuzzy mind. "When?"

She'd forgotten the question, and moving her head from side to side, she frowned and murmured, "What?"

"Your abortion, Micki," Wolf urged, his voice sounding strange. "When did you have it?"

The mistiness was clearing now, and opening her eyes, Micki stared in confusion into Wolf's pale face. He looked strained with white shadowy lines around his mouth.

"When, Micki?" The tone of his voice flicked at her like a lash.

"While I was still in college," she answered honestly, actually afraid to lie to him. "Six years ago."

CHAPTER 9

"Six years ago?"

The question emerged softly through lips that barely moved. Wolf was absolutely still for long, frightening moments then, his hands grasping her arms painfully, he pulled her to her feet to face him.

"You got rid of my baby?" he whispered hoarsely. When she didn't answer at once, he began to shake her hard. Fear closed her throat, making it almost impossible for her to answer. Feeling the faintness closing in on her again, she forced two words past the fear.

"Wolf, please."

He didn't even hear her. His face a terrifying mask of rage, he shook her harder and shouted, "You killed my baby?"

With a low moan Micki welcomed the blackness that covered her mind, blanking out the harsh sound of Wolf's voice.

When she opened her eyes again, she was lying on her bed. Wolf was sitting on its edge bending over her, his silvery eyes cold and blank. The expression of contempt on his face sent a shudder rippling through her and she began to shake. When he moved, her heart thumped wildly, and when his hands again grasped her arms, she brought her palms up against his chest, pleaded, "Wolf, please."

Before he could speak or even move, there was a loud exclamation from the doorway.

"Micki, Wolf!" Bruce said sharply. "What in the hell's going on here?"

Micki froze, her mind, her whole body seemingly turned to stone. His face becoming amazingly calm, Wolf released her and stood up with an easiness that was contradicted by the tenseness she could feel in him.

"Not what you apparently think," he replied smoothly. "Micki fainted."

Bruce obviously didn't believe Wolf, for he snapped, "You have no right in Micki's room."

"Not yet," Wolf returned. "But I will have very soon. Micki and I are going to be married."

"No!"

"Married!"

Micki's choked whisper went unheard, covered as it was by her father's loud exclamation.

"Yes." Wolf's flat tone held a ring of finality and the icy silver glance he threw at her told her he'd listen to nothing from her.

Panicstricken, Micki moved to get up to run to her father for protection, but the look of delight on his face stopped her.

"Wolf, that's great news." Smiling broadly, hand extended, Bruce walked to Wolf and clasped his hand warmly. "I couldn't be more pleased." Losing its brightness, his smile turned rueful. "I must admit that, for a minute there, I thought you—"

"We *have* been lovers, Bruce." Wolf's cool tone sliced across Bruce's words.

In shocked disbelief Micki's eyes darted from Wolf to her father, who looked, for a moment, like a time bomb ready to go off. His eyes had a murderous gleam and a muscle in his jaw twitched from the pressure of his clenched teeth. Was Wolf trying to get himself killed? What had possessed him to say such a thing? Trying to ward off the fight she felt sure was coming, Micki rushed into speech.

"Dad, let me explain." Micki scrambled off the bed and ran to her father, placing a detaining hand on the bunched-up muscle in his arm. "It happened—" That was as far as she got.

"It happened," Wolf repeated her words with cold finality, "because we both wanted it to happen." Ignoring her gasp, he stared coolly into Bruce's furious eyes. "Cool off, Bruce. So, okay, we didn't wait for the words, the ring, the document." He paused, then underlined, "Did you?"

The question caught Micki by surprise and in unwilling curiosity she glanced at her father's face.

"No."

Even though the light of battle had gone out of Bruce's eyes and Micki could feel the tension easing in his arm, Bruce had not given the answer. The softly spoken word had come from Regina who stood, until now unnoticed, in the doorway. Bruce turned his head to gaze for several seconds into his wife's composed face then, turning back to Wolf, Bruce echoed honestly, "No, we didn't wait."

"I *am* going to marry her, Bruce."

Wolf's statement, delivered with what Micki thought was overbearing confidence, vanquished what was left of her father's anger while at the same time igniting her own. Before she could voice her protest however, her father again clasped Wolf's hand.

"You've made your point, Wolf. I'm sorry if I came on a little heavily as the outraged father, but Micki's my only child and very important to me."

"I understand." Wolf accepted his surrender gracefully. "I'll take very good care of her, Bruce."

Feeling invisible, anger seethed inside Micki. Wasn't she going to be allowed to speak at all? Apparently not,

157

for before she could open her mouth, Regina suggested from the doorway, "We still have that bottle of champagne we were saving for a special occasion, Bruce. Don't you think this is the time to open it?"

"The perfect time," Bruce agreed, grinning broadly. "What are we standing here for? Let's go crack it open." He turned, began walking to the doorway, then, as if in afterthought, glanced back at Micki. "You feel all right now, honey?"

She wasn't even allowed to hand out her own health reports, for Wolf answered for her.

"She's fine now. I think the excitement got to her."

Excitement! You fatuous jerk, Micki thought furiously, *I'll excitement you!* Frustrated anger searing her throat, Micki watched her father drape his arm around Regina's shoulders as he left the room. The moment they were out of hearing she turned on Wolf.

"Have you gone mad?" Incensed, she spat the words at him. "I wouldn't marry you if I was ugly as sin and desperate. And, as you got yourself into this, you can damned well get yourself out of it. I'm going down there and stop them before they open that stupid bottle."

She spun away from him only to be spun right back again forcefully. Wolf's hand grasping her upper arm held her still. His voice, cold as ice, sent a chill skipping down her spine.

"No, you're not." His eyes bored into hers like steel drill bits. "You are going down there with me and accept their toast, and, as soon as they are back from the coast, you are going to marry me. You owe me."

"I owe you!" In her astonishment at his charge Micki missed the menace in his tone. "I owe you nothing."

"You owe me," he repeated coldly. "One child. When you produce that child, you may have your freedom."

Eyes widening in disbelief, Micki stared at him. He isn't mad, she thought wildly, he's a raving maniac. Fighting to control the renewed panic in her voice, she sneered,

"You have got to be kidding. There is no way I'd share a child with you."

"I didn't say share it," Wolf sneered back. "I said produce it. You chased my baby," he added crudely, "and you're going to damn well replace it."

"But that was six years ago!" Micki cried, not even attempting to correct him about how the child was lost.

"I don't give a damn if it was a hundred and six years ago. You're going to give me my child, my legitimate child. So stop arguing and let's go down and join the celebration." He started toward the door, dragging her with him. Before stepping through the doorway he paused, cocking one eyebrow at her. "Unless, of course, you want me to give your father—in minute detail—a blow-by-blow description of the weekend we spent together?" Again he paused before adding silkily, "And exactly how old you were at the time? You have"—he glanced at his watch unconcernedly—"fifteen seconds to decide."

A picture of her father's outraged expression of a few minutes ago followed by the fury he'd displayed about her being in Tony's apartment flashed through Micki's mind. Decide? What was to decide? She knew positively that should Wolf tell her father about that weekend their relationship would be irreparably damaged. Oh, he would not stop loving her, but he would never trust her again. The taste of defeat burning bitterly in her throat, she lashed out at him unthinkingly, "You rotten son-of-a—"

"Watch it." Wolf's warning, though soft, silenced her. Releasing her, he strode out of the room and along the hall. For one rebellious second Micki hesitated, then, hating herself, she hurried after him.

Wolf stayed long after the last drops of wine had been drained from the bottle. Stretched out lazily on a chair in the living room as if he belonged there, he smilingly lied through his teeth to her father and Regina.

Yes, he had been seeing Micki for some time, he assured them. And yes, they were both sure they did not want a large wedding. And no, unfortunately, they would not be able to get away on a honeymoon trip at this time, as, he was sure, Bruce and Regina could fully understand.

That part puzzled her. Why could her father and Regina fully understand that of all things? That question was answered for her after Wolf finally left, making a big production of drawing her out onto the porch with him, ostensibly to bestow a good-night kiss, in reality to warn: "Don't say anything stupid."

Flaming mad, Micki went back into the house prepared to take her chances and tell her father the truth. Her father's first words to her rang the death knell on that idea.

"You've made me very proud and happy, honey," he praised her seriously. "With the permissive attitude that seems to be the standard with young people today, well, I must admit I've had some very uneasy moments the last few years worrying about your future." Pausing to heave a sigh of relief, he grinned. "Like most fathers I hoped you'd marry well, but I've never dared to hope you'd do this well."

Her guns effectively spiked, Micki pondered his words in confusion. Somewhere along the road she had definitely missed something. Her father spoke as if he not only knew Wolf, but knew him well. And it was more than apparent that his opinion of Wolf differed vastly from Darrel's. Choosing her words carefully, Micki tried to close her intelligence gap.

"I'm relieved that you're pleased," she said slowly. "I was a little apprehensive about your reaction."

"Apprehensive?" Bruce's eyebrows shot up. "But why?"

"Well." Micki stole a glance at Regina. "He does have something of a reputation with women, doesn't he?"

"Micki," Regina inserted urgently before her father could answer. "Please let me explain."

"What's to explain?" Bruce waved his hand expressively. "So over the years he's been seen with a lot of different

160

women. He chose you. Good Lord, did you think I wouldn't realize what a compliment that is? The man is a millionaire several times over and a damned attractive one in the bargain. I'd have to be out of my mind to object to him as a son-in-law."

Micki's attention to her father's small speech ended with the words *millionaire several times over.* Wolf, a millionaire? Micki shuddered. Forcing herself to concentrate, she caught her father's last words.

"—and I have enormous respect for him. You just put your mind at rest about the other women, honey. At thirty-six he's obviously been waiting for the right woman. I'm delighted that woman is you."

What could she possibly say? There was no way she could look into his happy face and say, *Look, Dad, I hate to burst your bubble, but the threat of a firing squad wouldn't make me marry Wolf Renninger. Why? Because you see, Dad, he only wants me for the length of time it will take to produce one child. A child he mistakenly thinks I owe him. He may be wealthy and he may be attractive, but he is also vindictive and he wants what he believes is his due. And, Dad, I'm afraid that in the process he is going to tear me into tiny little pieces.* No, she very definitely could not say that.

What to do then? Micki shuddered. There was nothing she could say to him. Fatalistically Micki determined to give Wolf his due then run for what was left of her life. Hell, she shrugged mentally, everyone got divorced today anyway. Her mind made up, Micki pushed aside the small voice that cried, *That attitude may work for other people but not for you, it will destroy you.*

Presently the conversation switched from that of Micki's future wedding to the more immediate topic of Bruce and Regina's vacation trip. After receiving her father's repeated instructions on what to do if . . . with a gentle smile, Micki excused herself and went to her room. Convinced she wouldn't sleep, yet deciding she may as well be comfortable while awake, she had a tepid shower, slipped a nightie over her head, and slid between the sheets, where the exhausting events of the day caught up with her and she fell promptly asleep.

The morning was half gone before Micki woke. Feeling dull and still tired, she lay staring at the ceiling trying to come to grips with the unbelievable happenings of the night before. That Wolf was a millionaire was in itself plenty to think about, especially as she had begun to suspect Darrel was right in his assessment of him. But that her father obviously knew him much better than she did herself, and liked him as well, was almost too much to assimilate. How had they originally met? And not only how, but why had they become so well acquainted? Wolf had called her father Bruce. Not sir, or even Mr. Durrant, but Bruce, and to Micki that indicated a friendship, at least of sorts. Frowning, Micki got out of bed. She would simply have to ask someone.

She found that someone sitting at the kitchen table drinking coffee.

"Good morning, Micki." Pushing his chair back, Wolf rose to his feet, his eyes cautioning her to watch her reaction to his presence.

"Good morning," she managed huskily. "What are—I didn't expect to see you this morning."

"Wolf's going to drive us to the airport," Bruce said placidly. "He's got the motel station wagon."

"How nice," Micki cooed, looking away from the silvery eyes that sparked with fire at her tone. "And at exactly what time does the exodus begin?"

Unaccustomed to sarcasm from her, Bruce and Regina turned surprised eyes to her.

"Are you all right, princess?" Bruce asked, a frown creasing his forehead.

"Yes, of course, I'm sorry." Micki was instantly contrite. For heaven's sake, she chided herself, a sarcastic

162

mouth won't solve anything. Lowering her eyes, she murmured, "I think I'm missing you already, and you haven't even left yet."

"I knew it," Regina wailed in dismay. "I knew it was too soon after her homecoming to go away."

"No, Regina, really," Micki rushed to assure her. "I don't mind. I guess I'm still a little washed out from yesterday."

Bruce's eyes flicked from his wife to his daughter, an indecisive expression on his face. While Wolf sat silently, his eyes narrowing on Micki.

"Bruce," Regina said softly, "maybe with the wedding coming up this isn't the best time—"

"This is the perfect time," Wolf interrupted quietly. "If anyone has earned a vacation, you two have." His glance, cold and hard, sliced back to Micki. "You leave the 'princess' to me."

"We-ell, if you're positive," Bruce asked hopefully.

"I'm positive," Wolf replied in a hard tone. Then, his tone lighter, he grinned. "By the time you get back, all the arrangements will have been made and you can sit back and enjoy watching me hang myself."

Bruce and Regina returned his grin and the bad moment was past, except for Micki, who wanted very badly to slap Wolf's grinning face.

The jet made its charge down the runway and then it was airborne, its nose lifting regally toward the sky. Biting her lip, Micki watched the plane until it was swallowed up into the sun-splashed expanse of blue.

"Come on, Micki," Wolf chided dryly. "I'll take you home and let you cry on my shoulder."

Micki flinched away from his voice and the hand he placed at the back of her waist. Ignoring the hard thump her heart gave at the forbidding lines his face set into, Micki moved away from him quickly. At the car she again shook off his helping hand and slid onto the seat without looking at him. The way he palmed the gear lever as he shot out of the parking area told her clearly how angry she'd made him.

The silence was broken only one time on the drive back to her home. That was when he asked, "Would you like to stop for dinner?" And she answered, "No, thank you."

When he stopped the car in front of the house and reached for his door release, she said sharply, "Please, don't bother to get out. I'm tired, I have to work tomorrow and I'm going to bed."

His detaining hand prevented her from leaving the car. His voice low, almost pleasant, advised, "I think you should give a week's notice tomorrow."

"Give notice?" she repeated incredulously. "I'll do nothing of the kind. I have no intention of quitting my job."

"I won't have you working after we're married, Micki," he stated flatly.

"We're not married yet," she snapped. "Now let go of my arm, I want to go in."

Surprisingly he did, but she could feel his icy eyes boring into her back until she closed the front door and heard the car roar away from the curb.

The week that followed was nerve-racking for Micki. Business was slow at a time she very badly needed to keep busy. Wolf did not come to the house or call all week, and by Sunday night she had to mentally chide herself to stop pacing.

What was he trying to do? She had heard him tell her father that all the arrangements would be made when he and Regina got back and they would be home in one more week. Was he trying to upset her? Make her nervous? The questions tormented her as she paced from room to room, tired but too uptight to sit still.

Monday afternoon, busy at last checking over the arrival of a shipment of clothes purchased for the holiday

164

season, Micki went into the shop to question Jennell on an item, not bothering to look up when the door opened.

"On your toes," Jennell drawled softly. "The boss just walked in with a very enticing piece on his arm."

Glancing up, Micki felt her stomach flip and heard her breath hiss through her dry lips. Cool, relaxed Wolf walked toward her, his head bent slightly to one side as he listened to what the woman beside him said. A small smile playing at his lips, he nodded, then lifted his head to stare coolly into Micki's eyes.

"Hello, Jennell." Wolf's smile deepened. "This is Brenda Rider, Micki's replacement."

During the short, shocked silence that followed Wolf's announcement, Micki felt her hands go cold while her temper flared red hot.

"Micki's re—?" Jennell stopped short, her eyes flying to Micki's. "You're leaving?"

"Yes," Wolf answered for her. "To get married." A wicked light sprang into his eyes as he tacked on casually. "To me."

"Married!"

"Married!"

Jennell's outcry was echoed by Lucy, who at that moment came out of the stockroom to see what was keeping Micki.

"But she never said a word," Jennell moaned. Turning reproachful eyes on Micki, she asked. "Honey, why didn't you tell us?"

"I think I can answer that." Wolf again answered for her. "Micki wanted an easy, comfortable working relationship with you girls and she was afraid if she told you that would not be possible."

"Yes, I see," Jennell murmured, then, her eyes widening in alarm, she gasped. "Oh, Micki, that first day, I told you about—"

"It doesn't matter," Micki, fully aware that Jennell was referring to the previous buyer, cut in hastily. "It's of no

165

importance really." Ignoring the questioning look Wolf leveled at her, she turned to the woman with him. "How do you do, Brenda. I'm, as you heard, Micki and this is Jennell and Lucy." A small devil taking sudden possession of her, Micki lifted her hand, waved it in a shooing motion at Wolf and ordered, "Go away, Wolf, we'll take care of Brenda."

Another small silence followed Jennell's and Lucy's barely concealed gasps. Smiling sardonically, Wolf walked up to Micki, bent his head, and kissed her soundly on the mouth. When he lifted his head he grinned wickedly before, strolling to the door, he drawled, "You're the boss, baby—for now."

When she left the shop he was waiting for her, as she knew he would be. Falling into step beside her, he said, "We're having dinner together. I think it's time we talked."

He took her to a small, elegant, dimly lit dining room in another casino hotel. As it was still fairly early, only two of the room's tables were occupied, and given their choice of empty tables, Wolf indicated his preference for a secluded corner on the far side of the room. As they waited for their pre-dinner drinks, Micki's eyes scanned the room, the other diners, the black-jacketed waiter, everywhere but Wolf's face. When the drinks were served, Micki smiled vaguely at the waiter and studied his slender, retreating form, wondering irrelevantly if he had to lay flat on his back to close his skintight slacks.

"Now that you've done a complete inventory of the place and its occupants," Wolf inquired dryly, "do you think you could force your attention in this direction?"

Micki turned her head slowly, a disdainful expression on her face. Her icy glance didn't quite come off, however, as the flush that tinged her cheeks robbed it of its effect. Wolf, sipping at his Rob Roy, watched Micki intently, which deepened the heat in her face even more. Unable to maintain his narrow-eyed survey, Micki lowered her eyes to the frothy piña colada in front of her. His soft, weary-sounding sigh drew her eyes back to his.

"How did it go with Brenda this afternoon?" His even tone warned her he was just about at the end of his patience.

"Very well," she answered tightly, not even trying to hide her resentment. "As I'm very well aware you knew it would."

"Cool off, Micki," he advised softly. "We're not going to get anywhere if you blow your cork."

"What gives you the idea I want to get anywhere?" she asked coldly.

"Step down, honey," Wolf cautioned. "Okay, you're steamed, but damn it, Micki, I asked you to give notice. Why the hell didn't you?"

"I told you I didn't want to give up my job." Micki spat the words at him. "And I will not be ordered—" She broke off as the waiter approached their table to take their dinner orders. The minute he'd walked away again, Micki snapped angrily, "I will not be ordered around."

"And I told you I don't want my wife working," Wolf snapped back.

"I'm not your wife yet." Micki had to speak very softly to keep from shouting. "And I don't want—"

"I don't particularly care what you want," Wolf cut across her soft voice coldly. "It's done, you've been replaced, face it. Face this as well, there is no way you're getting out of this marriage, I want what's mine, and I usually get what I want."

"Spoken like a dyed-in-the-wool spoiled brat," Micki sneered. "It must be wonderful to be rich."

"It sure as hell beats being poor," Wolf taunted, his lips twitching with amusement. "I'll give you six months, then ask you if you agree." Then his face sobered and the near-smile disappeared. "You may have anything your tiny little heart desires as my wife, Micki."

For some reason the hard emphasis he'd placed on the

word *tiny* caused a sharp pain in the area mentioned. Hating the idea that he could hurt her so effortlessly, Micki taunted nastily, "In exchange for one child?"

"Precisely," Wolf answered coldly.

Once again they fell silent as the waiter served their meal. Staring at the food disinterestedly, Micki felt her eyes burning suddenly with a rush of memories. How totally different this was compared to the makeshift meals they had laughingly prepared and shared that long-ago weekend.

Automatically Micki put food in her mouth, chewed without tasting, desperately loving the Wolf she'd known then, desperately trying to hate the Wolf who sat opposite her now. When he spoke, his tone had thawed, but the taunting note remained.

"Would you care to hear my family's history?"

"If I must." Glancing up sharply, Micki leveled an accusing look at him. "I've been working for you right along, haven't I?"

"I honestly didn't know it, Micki." Wolf's tone held the clear tone of truth. "I seldom bother with the shops in any way. Not, that is, until the last few months."

"The previous buyer?" Micki asked oversweetly.

"The previous buyer," he agreed calmly. "She was no babe-in-the-woods; she knew the score. I suspect her vision was clouded by dollar signs. When she became possessive, I shipped her out." He paused, one brow raised as if asking if there were any questions. When there were none, he continued. "As I had done the shipping, I was given the job of replacing. I asked for a list of qualified possibles; your name was on it."

"You chose me deliberately?" she asked tightly, hating the thought of the previous buyer, yet refusing to let him know.

"Yes," Wolf answered bluntly.

"As a replacement in the store?" Micki asked smoothly. "Or—other places?"

168

"Don't push it, Micki," he warned softly.

"Okay." Micki backed off hastily. "Commence with the history."

"It's a long story," Wolf began. "But I'll cut it to the bone. It started with my great-grandfather who, as a young man, bought an inn with rooms for overnight guests along the Lancaster Pike near Lancaster, Pennsylvania. He prospered and as he did, he bought more inns and several small hotels in the southeastern part of the state. He was a rich man by the time he declared he was ready to retire. Leaving the running of his business in the capable hands of his only child, my grandfather, he grabbed his long-patient wife and took off for Florida."

Here his story was interrupted as the waiter came to clear the table and take their order for coffee and liqueurs. When that service had been completed, Wolf continued his narrative.

"Like most men who survive on work, he couldn't rest until he'd explored the possibilities in Florida. Before he died he'd acquired six hotels along the southeast coast. When he died he was a millionaire. My grandfather followed bravely in his footsteps. Deciding to take a chance, he invested heavily in a new type of travelers' accommodations: the motels. Payday, bonanza, and the whole bit. It was a smashingly successful venture."

Now he paused to light the darkest, slimmest cigar Micki had ever seen. After puffing contentedly several times, he resumed his tale.

"My grandfather's marriage had produced two sons. My father," he grinned, "Wolfgang the third, and my uncle Eric, who was ten years his junior. Eric was killed in the last days of Korea. His death triggered a heart attack that killed my grandfather a few months later. As Eric was childless, the growing monster, as we called the family business, went to my father. Here's where my mother enters the picture. Working beside him, she learned the business inside out. My father had one passion

169

besides my mother. He loved to sail. He was drowned, blown overboard, during a yacht race off the coast of South America. That left my mother and the rest of us to manage the business."

"The rest of you?" Micki probed.

"My father had better luck than his father and grand-father," Wolf supplied. "I have two brothers and a sister. My sister's the baby." Taking a test sip of his coffee, he glanced around the now-crowded room. "Family history to be continued," he said quietly. "Drink your coffee, Micki, and let's get out of here."

CHAPTER 10

They were quiet as they left the hotel, the quiet broken only when Wolf asked if Micki would like to gamble awhile before going home. Her only answer was a sharp shake of her head, which he accepted without comment.

"Go on with your story," Micki urged as soon as they'd left the heaviest traffic behind. "Or should I say your saga?"

"Got you interested against your will," Wolf taunted gently. "Didn't I?"

His soft, teasing tone did strange things to her breathing and for a flashing instant she ached all over for the feel of his arms around her. The mere thought of his mouth against hers drew a low moan from her throat that she somehow managed to turn into a whispered, "Yes."

"Where was I?" he asked himself. "Oh, yes, my brothers and sister. Eric is thirty-four, dark, unbelievably handsome and married to a rather plain, incredibly lovely young woman we all adore. They have two fair-haired, beautiful little girls. Eric takes care of the southeast, and now Honolulu, operations."

"Where does he live?" Micki asked when he stopped to draw a deep breath.

"Near Miami," Wolf replied. "Brett is thirty-one, taller than I, very slim, fair like our mother, not quite as handsome as Eric, and married one year to a vivacious red-headed ex-airline stewardess. They have no children—too busy having fun. They live in Atlanta. Brett handles things in the mid-Atlantic coastal area. While I, as you've probably figured out by now, take care of the northeast coastal area business."

Wolf grew quiet as he lit another cigar. Deciding she liked the strong, aromatic odor of the tobacco, Micki inhaled slowly before enquiring. "Is your mother retired?"

"My mother?" Wolf laughed. "Hardly. At sixty-one, she is still beautiful, energetic, and she holds the reins on the rest of us with iron control. She saw the potential in condominiums a long time ago. It was through her that the company branched out to include them. Now"—he shot her a smile that made her heart skip—"I've covered everyone but Diane. As I stated, Di is the baby of the outfit. She just turned thirty. She's blond, a beautiful reflection of our mother, and every bit as headstrong. When she finished college, she told mother she wanted to work but she wanted to do something different." He threw her a what-can-I-tell-you look. "Mother listened to her ideas, thought about it all of ten minutes, then, presto, we're in the boutique business. Di worked like hell in the shops until going into semi-retirement when her first child was born five years ago, she has two boys. Di and her husband also live near Miami, as does our mother. Her husband took on the mantle of manager."

"Hank Carlton," Micki inserted his name.

"Yes." They had been parked in front of her home for several minutes. Now, stepping out of the car, Wolf finished. "And there you have it. Any questions?"

"Yes," Micki answered, sliding off the seat. "Several."

"How about posing them over a cold drink?" he chided softly when she'd stopped short at the door. "All that talking has dried me out."

172

Micki stared at him for some moments before, giving in with a short nod, she unlocked the door and went in. Heading for the kitchen, she waved at the living room and murmured, "Make yourself comfortable. I can't offer you a Rob Roy, will scotch and soda do?"

"Plain water," he called after her. "Two ice cubes."

When she went into the living room, his drink in one hand, a glass of iced tea for herself in the other, he was sitting on the sofa, long legs stretched out in front of him, his head back, eyes closed. He had removed his jacket and tie and had opened the first three buttons of his shirt and the sheer, masculine sight of him sent a shaft of longing through her that was so intense her hands trembled. His eyes opened at the tinkling sound made by the ice tapping the insides of the glasses. Straightening, he took the glass she extended, patted the cushion beside him, and said, "Light and fire away."

Micki sat in the very center of the cushion, then stared into her glass to avoid looking into Wolf's amusement-filled eyes.

"How and when did you meet my father?" she blurted suddenly.

"I met him a few months before I met you." Although Wolf's tone was serious, it held a fine thread of laughter. "He handled the real estate transaction on the property where the motel now stands. He has been involved in every one of our property transactions in this area since then."

Micki turned wide, astonished eyes to him. "The big deal they were celebrating Saturday a week ago, that was yours?"

"The company's," he corrected gently. "Yes. And the big deal concerned not only another motel in the area, but a condominium in Cape May as well. Your father, several other realtors, and I had our work cut out for us talking Bianca Perriot out of the land the condo's going up on. Over six years of work as a matter of fact."

"Bianca Perriot?" Micki repeated faintly, a sick feeling invading her stomach.

"You remember, you met her a few weeks ago," Wolf prompted.

"Yes, of course, a lovely woman." Micki hesitated, but she had to ask, had to know. "You said over six years ago?"

Nodding, Wolf smiled ruefully. "The property had been in her husband's family for years. She wasn't sure if she should let it go." His tone took on a bitter edge. "She's the person I had an appointment with the day I brought you home from the boat. She batted all of us back and forth like tennis balls until a few weeks ago. It was motels and condos that brought me into this area in the first place."

Feeling foolish and stupid for the suspicions she'd harbored about Bianca, Micki was only too glad to change the subject.

"Brought you from where?"

"I was fairly well established in a New York office when I received orders from H.Q. to scout out the possibilities along the south Jersey coast," Wolf enlightened her. "At first I sent my assistant, whose reports were not very promising. I relayed the reports to H.Q. and received in reply just eight words. They were *If you want a job done right, move.* I moved."

Unable to believe anyone would dare issue an order like that to him, let alone that he'd meekly obey it, Micki stared at him in wide-eyed wonder.

At the look of shocked incredulity on her face, Wolf threw his head back and roared.

"Oh, honey," he finally managed between gasps for breath. "I assure you I did—post-haste. When that chairlady of the board gives an order, people better jump, most especially her sons. Since she took over, she has nearly tripled the company's combined income. No one argues with her."

"I see," Micki said softly, then a trifle fearfully, "and will I be expected to meet this business wizard?"

"Most certainly," he grinned. "She's looking forward to it breathlessly. But don't let the thought throw you, it's only her sons she cracks the whip at. Away from the office she's the most charming woman you could meet and a very understanding mother-in-law to my brothers' wives."

"You said," Micki rushed in as soon as he'd finished, "she's looking forward to meeting me. She knows about me?"

"Of course," Wolf answered easily. "I told her I was getting married when I flew to Miami to fill her in on the latest developments here." He paused before adding sardonically, "I was gone all last week—in case you hadn't noticed."

Micki felt her cheeks grow warm at the piercing look he gave her, and trying to hide her nervousness, she jumped up and asked, "Can I get you another drink?"

"No, thank you." Wolf's tone had changed. All business now, he went on briskly. "Sit down, Micki, we have plans to make."

"What plans?" Micki asked sharply, sitting down on the exact same spot she'd just vacated.

"You know damned well what plans," Wolf sighed tiredly. "I told your father that everything would be taken care of by the time he and Regina got home and I intend to see that everything is." His tone went brisk again. "Now we can do this the easy way, or we can do it the hard way, but, either way, it will be done. So, if you have any preferences, let's hear them."

"Like what, for instance?"

"Damn it, Micki." Wolf stood up abruptly, as if having to get away from her, and strode across the room. Turning suddenly, he raked his long-fingered hand through his hair and barked, "You know like what. Like do you want a church wedding with all the attendant hoopla, or would you prefer something more simple? If you want a big

175

splash, we have got to get it together. As I understand it, a large wedding takes several months to arrange. Personally I'd just as soon get it over with. The sooner the better."

Subdued by his outburst, Micki sat silent so long Wolf growled, "For chrissake, Micki, talk to me or I'll go ahead on my own and make all the arrangements."

"You seem to forget," Micki shouted at him. "I don't want to get married at all."

Striding back across the room, Wolf bent over her and said harshly, "I haven't forgotten a thing. Not one single thing. Do you understand?"

Cringing back into the sofa, Micki whispered, "Yes, damn you." Closing her eyes against the hard glitter in his, she added, "Make any plans you like. It means nothing to me."

She felt him move closer to her, felt his warm breath whisper over her skin an instant before his mouth covered hers. Steeling herself against an onslaught, she was completely undone by the gentleness of his kiss. His lips explored hers tenderly, coaxing them apart as he sat down beside her and drew her gently into his arms. Determined to remain cold in his arms, Micki groaned with dismay when her mouth, then her body, responded hungrily to his. Bringing her hands up to his chest to push him away, her fingers, as if with a mind of their own, sought his warm skin at the opening of his shirt. She was trembling on the brink of surrender when he lifted his head and whispered, "I think I'll very much enjoy making you eat your words. But don't worry about it, I'll sweeten them for you."

Shocked into cold reality by his taunt, Micki pushed at his chest. Breathing harshly, she growled, "Get out of here. I don't want you to touch me or even look at me. You sicken me."

Anger flared in his eyes before his narrowed lids concealed it. Rising to his feet in a quick, fluid movement, he picked up his jacket and headed for the door tossing over his shoulder, "I'll call you when the arrangements are completed."

"Drop dead," Micki called after him, feeling very childish when she heard his mocking laughter.

Micki heard nothing from him until Friday morning. During the interval she received three post cards from her father and Regina, alternately extolling the beauties of the West Coast and their growing excitement about her marriage. Moodily, she'd considered jumping off the Ninth Street Bridge.

Wolf's first words to Micki when she answered the phone Friday morning were "I'll pick you up in half an hour. We're going for the license."

Three hours later they were back at the house, everything taken care of. They would be married, Wolf had informed her coldly, late Tuesday afternoon. It would be a civil ceremony, no fuss, no bother. Even the witnesses would be impersonal county employees.

Wanting to weep and forcing herself not to, Micki held her head high and snapped, "That's fine with me," and walked into the house, forcing herself not to run.

Panic built steadily during the rest of that day and all day Saturday. Sunday brought relief in the form of her father and Regina's return, and chagrin in the form of Wolf's arrival at the house soon afterward.

For several hours Micki managed to avoid speaking directly to Wolf. Intent on keeping her father and Regina talking, she coaxed an almost hour-by-hour description of their activities from them. Finally, unable to pull one more question from her mind, Micki grew silent and tense.

"Now that my inquisitive offspring has apparently run down," Bruce laughed teasingly, "perhaps one of you will answer a few questions for me."

Leaving Wolf to the answering, Micki went to the sink to make a pot of fresh coffee, and as it was already past dinnertime, to prepare a light supper of salad and sandwiches.

Both Bruce and Regina voiced protest at the meager wedding plans. Wolf listened to all their arguments patiently but remained adamant in his resolve to go through with them as stated. The shuffling around as Micki served the hastily put together meal ended the argument. By the time Wolf left, Bruce and Regina had resigned themselves to the inevitable.

Monday morning, Labor Day, Micki stared out her bedroom window at the bright, hot day, and wished she'd accepted Cindy's invitation to join them for a barbecue. Sighing at the memory of Cindy's excitement on hearing that Micki was getting married, she turned listlessly when Regina entered the room.

"We have really got to talk now, Micki," Regina said nervously, "about Wolf, and what happened six years ago."

"I don't see what good—"

"Maybe none," Regina interrupted, closing the door. "I'm afraid I made a bad error in judgment that day."

"Error in judgment?" Micki repeated blankly. "In what way?"

"In the depth of your feelings for Wolf. I thought you an immature teenager infatuated with an older, exciting man. And it wasn't like that, was it? You were very much in love." Without waiting for Micki to comment she went on. "You still are."

"Am I?" Micki asked carelessly.

"Your cool facade doesn't fool me, Micki," Regina chided. "I've watched you ever since you came home. As much as you try to hide it, you light up at the mere mention of his name."

"Why are you doing this, Regina?" Micki whispered.

"Because I must," she answered tightly. "Because I can't let you marry him thinking there had been something between us. There wasn't."

Micki went cold. Then she got hot, blazingly hot.

178

"Then why did you infer that there was?" Micki asked bitingly. "What was the purpose?"

"I thought I was protecting you," Regina explained. At the look of disgusted disbelief that crossed Micki's face, Regina insisted. "I truly was, Micki. Wolf had been involved with several women that I knew of. But they were mature women able to take care of themselves. You were only nineteen, and when I saw that mark on your neck—" Regina shrugged. "I just felt I had to do something to keep you from getting hurt."

"But I heard you talking to him on the phone," Micki argued.

"On the phone?" Regina looked blank, then confused. "But as far as I can remember, all we talked about was real estate. I had gone to New York with your father against Wolf's advice, and he as much as said I told you so. He had stayed to talk to Bi—"

"I know," Micki cut in weakly.

Later, after Regina left, Micki paced her room like a caged tiger. Six years! The words hammered in her brain. She had run away for nothing! What a fool she'd been! What a child! All this time she could have been with him. That thought brought her to a standstill. But could she? Wolf had had, did have, a reputation with women. How long would she have lasted before he shipped her out of his life? But she had been carrying his child. That he would have wanted. That he still wanted. And that, she thought sadly, was all he wanted.

Even so, she faced Tuesday morning with hope. Wolf had said she could have her freedom after she'd produced a child, but maybe, just maybe, she could make him change his mind. She loved him. She had to try and make him love her too.

Palefaced and trembling in her off-white shantung sheath, Micki stood beside a pearl-gray-suited Wolf and repeated the traditional vows.

The one concession her father had won from Wolf was

179

that he and Regina would take Micki and Wolf for dinner after the ceremony. He chose a well-known restaurant in Wildwood where, over bright red lobsters, he solemnly lifted his glass of champagne and wished them happiness. Wolf was pleasant and amusing and Micki was trembling with nervousness.

The dinner seemed unending but finally it was over. Her stomach churning, Micki added very little to the banter that flew back and forth between Wolf and her father and Regina as they drove back up the coast.

They were met at the motel by the manager, who wished them smiling congratulations, and a grinning good night. Wolf was quiet as they walked up the stairs and along the hall, so quiet Micki felt all her nerves tighten. The minute he closed the door, she made for the window like a homing pigeon.

"Would you like something to drink?" Wolf's voice came to her from the direction of the kitchen.

She had eaten very little all day, had barely touched her dinner, and had had three glasses of champagne but she said, "Whatever you're having," hoping it would calm her nervousness. She turned as he strolled into the room, a glass in each hand.

"That's a fantastic view," she murmured breathlessly, taking the glass he extended.

"There's one exactly like it in the bedroom," Wolf drawled softly, his eyes lingering on her lips.

Suddenly parched, Micki lifted her glass and drank thirstily, then, her throat on fire, her eyes smarting, she gasped, "What is that?"

"Scotch and water," Wolf laughed softly. "You did say whatever I was drinking."

"Yes," she exhaled deeply. "But if you don't mind, I don't think I can finish this." She handed the now-half-empty glass back to him and turning, added jerkily, "I—I think I'll have a shower."

Forty-five minutes later, clothed only in the filmy nightgown and matching peignoir that had been a bridal gift from her father and Regina, Micki stood in her bare feet, staring out the huge square bedroom window that looked out over the beach and ocean. The bedroom was decorated in the same earth tones as the living room, the furniture modern with straight, clean lines.

Hearing the shower shut off, she shivered and curled her toes into the soft fiber of the carpet. Wolf had come into the room while she was brushing her hair and, with hardly a glance at her, had gone directly into the bathroom. When the bathroom door opened, she closed her eyes. The thick carpet muffled Wolf's light tread and when his finger touched her shoulders she jumped, startled.

"Relax, honey." Wolf's warm breath ruffled the hair at her temple. "This isn't going to hurt a bit."

His hands moving slowly, he slid the peignoir over her shoulders and down her arms to her hands, where the garment dropped soundlessly to the floor. She shivered as his fingers trailed back up her arms to the ribbon bows on her shoulders that kept the gown in place. His lips teasing the sensitive skin behind her ear, his fingers tugged open the bows and the sheer gown slithered sensuously down her body.

For tormenting moments his hands caressed her shoulders, her throat, before he turned her slowly to face him. Raw desire shimmered darkly in his silvery eyes. As he bent his head to hers, Micki, torn between apprehension and anticipation, breathed.

"Oh, Wolf."

Expecting the searing brand of his mouth, Micki closed her eyes. His lips barely touched hers. Light as down he brushed her mouth with his, again and again, slowly building in her a need for his kiss. Adding to the tantalizing touch of his lips, his fingertips drew maddeningly fine lines down the side of her neck. When the tip of his tongue danced along her lower lip, she moaned with the urgency only this man could arouse in her.

181

With a small sob she coiled her arms around his neck and at that moment his mouth crushed hers, while his arms, encircling her body, drew her close to him. His kiss was hard, demanding and giving at the same time, and Micki gave herself up to the sheer joy of it.

Without breaking the kiss, Wolf straightened. His arms, holding her tightly, drew her up with him, then, her toes dangling inches above the floor, he carried her to the side of the bed. Sliding her body against his, he set her back on her feet. Wordlessly he lowered her to the bed and stretched his long length beside her.

All thought ceased for Micki. All she wanted was the feel of his mouth, his hands, his body. It had been so very, very long, and she loved him so very, very much.

Wolf's mouth played with hers, teasing her, delighting her. His tongue pierced and explored while his hands caressed and grew bold, exciting her to the edge of endurance. When his lips left hers she threw back her head to give him access to her throat. Making a moist path, his lips moved down the arched column to the hollow at its base where he paused to explore with his tongue, then, moving on, his lips climbed the soft mound of her breast to its summit, closed around its hard peak.

Micki was unaware of the soft moaning sounds she was making deep in her throat until Wolf, returning to kiss and tongue-tease her neck near her ear, whispered, "That's right, honey, purr for me. Purr like the amoral little cat you are."

It took ten full seconds for his words to sink in and when they did Micki froze.

"What did you say?" Her voice sounded loud after the murmurings of lovemaking.

"I think you heard me." Lifting his head, Wolf looked at her coolly.

"You think I'm immoral?"

"Not immoral, honey, amoral," he corrected. "Like a cat that doesn't know any better."

"Let me go," Micki whispered around the pain in her throat. "I said let me go," she snapped when he made no move to obey. "I don't want you."

"Oh, but you do, and I know it," Wolf whispered. "I'm a male and that's all that's required, isn't it?"

Micki didn't think; she reacted. Curling her hand into a small fist she lifted her arm and punched him right in the mouth. Wolf's head jerked back and then he laughed.

"I really am going to enjoy making you eat your words and anything else that comes to mind."

Moving swiftly he caught her mouth with his, kissing her sensually, erotically until she was breathless and had stopped struggling against him. Then with slow deliberation, using all the expertise he possessed—and that was considerable—he set a blaze burning inside her that only one thing would quench. His own breathing ragged, he growled, "I'll make you forget Tony, and Baxter and God knows how many others. By the time I'm through with you, no other man will ever satisfy you. You may hate me everywhere else, but you'll beg for me in bed."

"No." Micki's head moved from side to side. What did he mean Tony and Baxter and the many others? Surely he didn't think . . .

"Wolf, no, I—"

"Yes," Wolf rasped against her mouth, silencing her.

It was past noon when Micki woke up. She was alone in the bed, and, if the still quiet was any indication, in the apartment. Turning her head wearily on the pillow, she gazed out the huge window at yet another blatantly blue sky. Now, in early September, after a long summer filled with blatantly blue skies, Micki wished for chill, cloudy days to match her mood.

Stirring restlessly, she closed her eyes. Where the hell were all the cold, rainy days people were always singing about? Spreading her fingers, she smoothed her palm over the sheet where Wolf had lain, humiliating heat warming her body. He had made good his threat—several times over. She had not only welcomed him she had urged him to join with her; she had literally begged.

With a groan she rolled over, her body replacing her hand on the now-cool sheet, her face burrowing into the indentation Wolf's head had made in the pillow.

Curling into a tight ball, she wept the tears of the damned. He had stripped her of all pride, all pretense. Inside her head she could hear the echo of her own damnation.

"Wolf, please—please," she had pleaded.

"You'll have to do better than that," Wolf had taunted.

"What do you want of me?" she'd wept.

"Everything," he'd growled harshly. "Your body, your soul, your mind. I'd ask for your heart, but I know you don't possess one."

That, more than anything that followed, had hurt her the most. He thought her amoral. A hedonistic little alley cat incapable of deep affection or love. A hard shudder shook her body. She had made one attempt to tell him how she felt. Nearly incoherent, sobbing into his shoulder, she'd pleaded, "Wolf, please, don't do this to me. I love you."

Wolf had become still for a moment, and then his harsh laughter struck her with more force than if he'd used his fist on her.

"Oh, sure," he'd taunted coldly. "Me and Tony and Baxter and probably every other male you've ever met in between. Save your love song for the naive ones. I don't need or want it. But I do want everything else. So coax me, honey. Change your love song to a lust song and I just might hear you."

And all the time he'd been inflicting those hurtful words on her he'd also been inflicting an exquisite brand of torture. With his hands, with his mouth, with his entire body, he had pushed her up one side of the mountain called desire and chased her down the other side.

Mindless, lost, and groping in the world of the senses

he'd created around her, she had clutched at him, pleading, sobbing, begging him to find her, save her.

And when, finally, he had, not once, but over and over again, she had completed her own damnation by humbly thanking him.

Now, alone, eaten alive by a love that no amount of humiliation could change into anything else, Micki wept into the pillow that still held his spicy, masculine scent.

By the time Wolf returned to the apartment, most of the day was gone—as were all traces of the tears she'd shed.

Barefoot, dressed in jeans and a cotton pullover, Micki sat curled up in a chair, an unlooked-at magazine on her lap.

Coming to a stop three feet in front of her chair, Wolf, looking drawn and bone tired in an obviously hand-tailored business suit, studied her makeup-free face broodingly.

"How young you look," he said softly. "Young and innocent and untouched."

"Wolf."

Her anguished cry seemed to snap something inside of him. Flinging himself into the chair opposite hers, he closed his eyes and massaged his forehead with his fingertips. As his hand moved, he raked his fingers through his hair and looked up at her.

"I'm sorry, baby." His voice was raw and soft. "I've had one hell of a day reliving all I said to you, did to you last night. And the damning thing is I meant to do it. Planned to do it."

"Why, Wolf?" Micki whispered brokenly.

"Because I couldn't stand the thought of all those other men," he replied harshly. "Or that you had rejected my child." His eyes, glinting with resentment and anger, pierced hers. "You didn't have to get rid of it, Micki. All you had to do was call me." His voice went raw with emotion. "I'd have taken care of you. I wanted to take care of you."

185

"But, Wolf, I—"

"You had no right, damn you." Wolf's stinging words cut across hers as if he hadn't heard her. "You had no right to have it scraped from your body like a detested growth."

"Wolf, stop," Micki commanded in sudden anger. "I—oh!" With a gasp she cringed back against the chair, for Wolf had jumped to his feet, crossed the space between them, and stood looming over her.

"Stop, hell," he snarled. "Let's have it out in the open. It's been festering in my guts long enough. I'd have kept it, Micki. I thought that weekend was beautiful and to have a child from it would have made it perfect."

Really afraid of him now, yet unwilling to admit it even to herself, Micki glared up at Wolf and challenged him. "Are you going to beat me, Wolf?"

"Beat you?" Wolf frowned, then followed her eyes as they dropped to his tightly clenched fists. Sighing deeply, he backed up, his fingers slowly uncurling. "No, Micki." He smiled ruefully as he lowered his body wearily into the chair. "I did enough damage to you last night without taking my fists to you." His eyes flashed briefly. "But I felt I had to obliterate in my mind as well as yours the memory of all those other men."

Hot, swift anger seared through Micki's mind. He had said those words one too many times.

"Goddamn you, Wolf, there were no other men!" Micki cried. "There has never been any other man." With a sudden violence that startled him, she flung the magazine across the room and said bitterly, "And I didn't kill or get rid of or chase your baby." The spurt of fire died as quickly as it had flared, leaving her pale face with a haunted look. "I wanted your baby, Wolf." Her voice was husky with remembered pain. "I wanted it desperately. I lost it."

"But you said abortion." Wolf's tone revealed his mental torment. "Your exact words were, 'I haven't felt this bad since the abortion,' don't lie to me, Micki, not now."

"Yes, I said abortion, because that is the correct term." Wolf winced and she added strongly. "That is the correct medical term, Wolf. I did not reject your baby, my body did."

The eyes that stared into hers lost their silver clarity and grew uncertain with doubt. Her eyes filled with tears.

"I don't have to lie to you, Wolf. Go to the hospital. Check the records," she urged. "If the doctor that took care of me is still there, talk to him." Her voice caught on a sob, and brushing the tears from her cheek, she whispered, "I held the thought of your baby very closely, Wolf. Losing it was like losing part of myself."

Wolf was quiet a long time and Micki watched, her bottom lip caught between her teeth, as the clouds of doubt left his eyes.

"Good God!"

The whispered words were more a plea than a curse. Dropping his head back onto the chair, he stared through the window at the sky. When his eyes came back to hers, the silver had changed to a bleak gray.

"Why did you run away from me six years ago, Micki?" he asked wearily. "Was I too old for you? Had I frightened you?"

"No!" Micki exclaimed.

"Then why?" he demanded. "For six years I've asked myself that question. Why, after that fantastic weekend, had you run? When I came for you that night I wanted to give you"—his hand waved in an encompassing circle —"everything. Damn it, Micki, I was prepared to do anything to keep you with me. I wanted to marry you so badly my teeth hurt with the wanting." His tone went ragged. "Why did you run?"

Tears stinging her eyes, Micki swallowed against the tightness in her throat and whispered, "I thought you were having an affair with Regina."

"WHAT!"

The word seemed to bounce off the walls.

"I know, now, that it wasn't true," Micki said quickly. "But for six years I thought it was. And I couldn't stay with you thinking you and she had—" Micki shuddered.

"God," Wolf groaned, then, "Tony?" Before she could reply he added harshly, "How I hated that name. It seemed every time I called you all I heard was that name. Tony. Tony. Tony. Even when I mentioned your name in the shop I heard, 'She's in Albany with Tony.' Were you?"

"I went to Albany to attend Tony's wedding," Micki said quietly. "He's a friend. A very good friend. Nothing more."

"And Baxter?"

"Darrel asked me to marry him," she explained. "I said no. And as for any others over the years, casual dates, all of them."

"Come here to me, babe," Wolf coaxed, holding out his arms to her. "You can do whatever you like when you get here. Kiss me, punch me in the mouth again, anything. But come let me hold you."

Jumping out of her chair, Micki ran to him, snuggled into his arms.

"We make a pair," he murmured into her hair. "Me, going out of my mind thinking you're jumping in and out of bed with every guy you meet. And you, eating your heart out because you believed I was sleeping with your stepmother, and God knows how many others. Oh, yes, we make a fine pair. We deserve each other."

"Don't we though?" She laughed up at him.

There is something incongruous about grocery bags sticking out of an open Ferrari, thought Micki suddenly while she lifted the bags off the seat. A small smile curving her lips, she closed the car door with a quick sideways thrust of her hip.

Wolf, waiting at the open kitchen door of the large beachfront rancher, relieved her of her burden with a terse, "Where the hell have you been all this time? Your

188

father and Regina and my mother and the rest of the clan will be here in less than two hours."

"I know, I'm sorry," Micki apologized, dropping her glasses, keys, and handbag onto a chair. "The store was packed," she explained, beginning to empty the bags he'd placed on the table. "And the checkout lines didn't seem to move." She sighed. "And then I ran into Mrs. Jenkins and she talked and talked and—"

"Somewhat like you're doing right now?" Wolf asked dryly.

"Oh, Wolf—" Micki began, then broke off, alarm-filled eyes flying to his at a loud wail from the interior of the house. "Is something wrong with Cub?" she asked anxiously.

"No, of cour—" Another wail reached them.

Dropping the box of snack crackers she was holding, Micki started for the doorway, only to be brought up short by Wolf's hand grasping her wrist.

"Cub is fine," he said firmly. "The nurse is giving him his bath." He grinned. "And you know how much he loves that."

Micki sighed with relief, then gave a gasped "oh" when Wolf, with a quick tug at her wrist, pulled her against him. Holding her loosely in his arms, he complained, "Cub is fine, but I'm feeling neglected." Bending his head, he caught her lips in a light kiss that very quickly turned into a hungry demand.

Bemused, lost in the scorching wonder of Wolf's mouth, Micki was raising her arms to circle his neck when another irritated wail brought her to her senses. Sliding her mouth from his, she scolded, "Wolf, stop it. What if your mother should walk in right now?"

"She'd understand perfectly," Wolf replied blandly. "And say I was a true Renninger," he teased. "Mother's been over that mountain."

Feeling her cheeks go pink, Micki made a move to break

189

free of his arms. All she accomplished was to find herself held more tightly against him.

"You look tired," he murmured. "I think you should go lie down for a half hour or so. If you like, I'll come with you, rub your back." His eyes gleamed wickedly. "And your front."

While he was speaking, his right hand was moving. Under her sweater, up her side and, on his last word, over her breasts. Even through the lacy material of her bra the hardening tip his fingers found, caressed, proclaimed the effect he was having on her.

Stepping away from her suddenly, he clasped her hand and strode through the room, taking her with him.

"Wolf, the groceries!" Micki yelped, practically running to keep up with him.

Without breaking stride, he growled softly, "That's what I pay a housekeeper for."

When he reached the master bedroom with its wide, sliding glass doors facing the ocean, he swung her inside, slammed the door, and said softly, "We have two hours before the horde descends on us for the birthday party for the Wolf's cub." His eyes caressed her, inflaming her senses. Without conscious thought her fingers went to the zipper on her skirt. Silvery eyes followed her hands and his voice went husky. "I've been waiting for you all afternoon, planning a party of our own."

Watching him yank his gray-and-white velour shirt over his head, desire flared inside Micki, sweeping all thoughts from her mind but one.

Within seconds the floor was littered with their clothing and they were on the large bed, mouth to mouth, flesh to flesh, together.

Her soft throaty moans inflaming him, Wolf husked, "Oh, God, I love you, baby. I love you."

Later, wrapped in Wolf's arms and the afterglow of their lovemaking, Micki sighed in contentment.

"After the way you celebrated your cub's birthday," she

teased softly, her hand stroking over his hip. "I can hardly wait to see what you have planned for our anniversary."

Fleetingly the memory of their wedding night invaded her mind and her hand paused in its caressing movement.

Wolf's soft laughter dissolved the memory. His hand covered hers, urging it onward on its journey down his long, taut thigh.

"Maybe I should put you in charge of planning that party," he murmured against her hair.

Tilting her head back, she looked up into his wickedly gleaming eyes.

"You're getting pretty inventive in that department." Dipping his head, he covered her invitingly parted lips with his own, his hand leaving hers to spread possessively, protectively over her still flat belly. When he lifted his head, his eyes traveled down her body to his hand.

"When are you going to make your announcement?"

"Oh, not until after Wolfgang has been duly honored," she grinned. "Do you think I should tell them I'm already positive this one's a girl? Wolf, what?"

Sitting up suddenly, Wolf had replaced his hand with his lips.

"I love you, my daughter," his warm breath fluttered across her skin, exciting her, warming her. "And I love your mama."

Micki felt tears sting her eyes even as her body moved sensuously under his mouth as he trailed his lips up to her throat.

"And I love her daddy," she whispered huskily, some long moments later.

LOOK FOR NEXT MONTH'S
CANDLELIGHT ECSTASY ROMANCES™

25   FREEDOM TO LOVE, *Sabrina Myles*
26   BARGAIN WITH THE DEVIL, *Jayne Castle*
27   GOLDEN FIRE, SILVER ICE, *Marisa de Zavala*